1959

The Gravedigger at work . . .

"I take it you don't want to go to jail, Mr. Smoot," Graves said, pulling black leather gloves tight on his hands.

"I'd rather not," said Smoot.

"You can leave it be, mister," said the U.S. marshal, "or you can drop your guns and join him. It's your choice."

"I think there's another choice," said the Gravedigger . . .

None of the witnesses could say which man went for his gun first. It was as if it happened while everyone on the street blinked at once. Both guns were out and flashing and barking. . . . A bullet from the marshal's gun ripped the hat off of Graves's head. Suddenly the shooting stopped. Both men were still standing, but a smear of blood began spreading over the white shirt and black vest of the agent. He was standing straight, his Colt held out in front of him, still pointed generally in the direction of the Gravedigger. His fingers relaxed and dropped the gun. His knees buckled, and he pitched forward, falling off the sidewalk and into the street. United States Marshal Dan "Road" Agent was dead.

JAKE LOGAN

SLOCUM
AND THE GRAVEDIGGER

JOVE BOOKS, NEW YORK

SLOCUM AND THE GRAVEDIGGER

A Jove Book / published by arrangement with
the author

PRINTING HISTORY
Jove edition / January 2002

Visit our website at
www.penguinputnam.com

ISBN: 0-515-13231-4

A JOVE BOOK®
Jove Books are published by The Berkley Publishing Group,
a division of Penguin Putnam Inc.,
375 Hudson Street, New York, New York 10014.
JOVE and the "J" design
are trademarks belonging to Penguin Putnam Inc.

PRINTED IN THE UNITED STATES OF AMERICA

10 9 8 7 6 5 4 3 2 1

1

Slocum suddenly felt himself flying through the air, but not freely, for he had no control. He had thought he was in control, thought he was doing just fine, but then he had been shot up into the air like a bolt. His feet lost the stirrups. His hands lost the reins. Most important and most frightening of all, his ass lost its seat in the saddle. He was airborne. He had gone up straight, or almost straight, but then he seemed to be moving forward, head first. He sailed over the head of the still madly leaping roan beneath him. The farther he soared, the more his head took the lead. The higher his feet went. Then as he at last started his descent, his head, still leading, moved lower than his ass and his feet. He was headed for the hard ground face first. Desperate, he tucked his chin into his chest, and just before he hit with an awful crash, he rolled just enough to land on his shoulders. Clouds of choking dust rose all around him.

He was aware of the activity surrounding him then. Men ran to gather around him, and voices asked in desperation after his health. At the same time others moved in on the rampaging stallion with blankets and ropes. Slocum caught his breath. "I'm all right," he said. Slowly he sat up. Then he stood. He dusted off the seat of his trousers. A cowboy standing nearby picked up his hat and handed it to him, and Slocum slapped it against his thigh, knocking loose the dust and dirt. He pulled it back down tight on his head and turned toward where the other men fought to control the angry roan stallion.

"Snub him back up, boys," Slocum said.

"Slocum," snapped a heavyset man sitting on the fence, "I told you no one could ride that roan, and now you seen first-hand how come me to say that. You don't mean to try it again?"

"We was just getting acquainted that first round," Slocum said. "I know him now all right. I'll ride him."

The roan was snubbed up close to the snubbing post, standing spraddle-legged and trembling, a blanket thrown over his head. Slocum walked over to its side.

"You sure?" a cowhand asked.

Slocum grabbed hold of the saddle horn and put a foot in a stirrup. He swung aboard.

"Let him go, boys," he said.

Surprised at his sudden freedom, the big horse reared. As his front hooves came down hard, the back ones kicked out. He jumped. He ran. He spun, first to the right, then to the left. He leaped to one side, then kicked back his rear legs and swung his rear end hard to the right. He tried every trick he had in his equine brain, but still the unwanted man sat on his back, still he held on. At last the big horse, blowing hard, slobbering, nearly exhausted, stopped jumping. Instead he ran. He ran around the edge of the corral fence. He ran as if he thought he could run out from under the man. After several rounds, he slowed to a trot. Slocum began to turn him this way and that. Soon he was riding the roan almost as if he had been riding it for months. A cheer went up from the cowboys around the corral.

Slocum dismounted and handed the reins to a waiting wrangler. He walked toward the heavyset man sitting on the fence.

"By God," the man said, "I was wrong. You sure enough rode that outlaw."

"He'll make a good horse," Slocum said. "You treat him right."

"Well," the man said, "that was your last one."

"Yes, sir," Slocum said. "Soon as you pay me off, I'll be riding out of here."

"Slocum," the man said, "I know you told me you meant to

move along soon as you busted that string, but if you was to change your mind, I've got a job for you."

"No, thank you, Mr. Bates," said Slocum. "I'm sticking to what I said. I think it's time for me to move on."

He wondered at himself. Bates was an easy man to work for, a good man. The pay was as good as any, and Slocum knew that what he had in his jeans, even after Bates paid him for busting the string of broncs, would not last him forever. He had no idea where he would get another job, had no idea, in fact, where he would go when he rode off the Bates place. There was only one reason for him to quit this job. He was footloose. He'd hung around one place for too long. He was growing restless.

Bates climbed down off the fence.

"Come along, Slocum," he said.

Slocum walked with Bates to the big ranch house and on inside through the front door. He stood politely, his hat in his hand, as Bates opened a cash box and counted out some bills. Then Bates handed the cash across the desk to Slocum.

"You're always welcome here, Slocum," he said.

"Thank you, Mr. Bates," Slocum said. "Well, I'll be seeing you."

He shoved the hat back onto his head and turned to leave the room. As he reached the door and was about to pull it open, Bates called out to him.

"Slocum," he said. "Good luck to you."

Slocum nodded and went on outside. Stuffing his money into his pocket, he stepped down off the porch and headed for the far end of the corral where his big Appaloosa waited patiently. The horse was already saddled, and the blanket roll was tied on behind the saddle. Slocum's Winchester was in the scabbard, and his Colt was in its holster, the belt buckled and slung over the saddle horn. He was packed and ready to go.

"Hey, Slocum," a voice called out. He looked and saw Sammy Golden running toward him, waving a paper in his hand. He stood and waited a moment until Golden ran up beside him and stopped, breathing deeply to catch his breath.

"What is it, Sam?" Slocum asked.

"This here letter I got." Golden panted. "Read it."

He held the letter out. Slocum hesitated, then took the letter and read it.

"Well, I'll be damned," he said. "Congratulations."

Golden grinned.

"Then it really says what I thought? I own a goddamn ranch?"

"That's what it says all right," Slocum said. "You're the sole heir, it says. And it's signed by this lawyer feller whose name is on the top of the paper. Jeremy Grimes, Attorney at Law. Sounds like a big spread too. Sammy, nine out of ten beat-up, old cowhands tells themselves they're going to own their own spread someday. Most never do. But you've got yours, old son. I'm real glad for you."

He started to walk on, but Golden grabbed his arm.

"Slocum."

"What?"

"Where are you going?"

Slocum gave a shrug.

"Just drifting," he said.

"Well, uh, would you drift along my way? Go with me to check out my new spread? Help me make sure it's going good? I'll pay you foreman's wages. I mean, I ain't got no money to speak of, but with a big spread like that, I ought to go to making some soon, hadn't I?"

"I'd say so."

"Well? Will you?"

Slocum rode south with Sammy Golden. Golden was so excited with his newly acquired property that he couldn't keep his mouth shut. He talked almost constantly. He knew the size of the ranch from Grimes's letter, but he wondered out loud how many head of cattle were grazing on it, how many horses. He supposed that the deceased previous owner had left behind a full crew of hands, and he wondered, still out loud, if they had all stayed on to await the arrival of the new owner. He wondered if they were good and loyal hands and if he would be satisfied with them and they with him.

"Golly, Slocum," he said, "I never thought of it till just now."

"Of what?" Slocum said.

"What if I have to fire someone? I ain't never done nothing like that. I don't think I'd be very good at it."

"That's why you have a foreman," said Slocum. "Let him do your dirty work for you."

"But what if I inherited a foreman, and I don't like him?"

"Let's just wait till we get there and see what happens," said Slocum.

They spent several days and nights together on the long trail, camping, hunting for food to supplement the meager trail fare, and Slocum decided that Sammy Golden was all right. Back at Bates's place, Slocum hadn't really grown to know Golden all that much. He was getting to know him on the trail though, the best and fastest way to get to know a man. And Sammy Golden, Slocum decided, was only just a man. He was game enough, but his experience of the world was limited.

It became apparent quickly enough, for instance, that Golden was afraid of taking over a large ranch. That was why he had practically begged Slocum to ride along with him. He was also ignorant of the ways of a dammed lawyer, but then Slocum figured that any man ought to stay wary when forced to deal with one of those shyster bastards.

All along the way, Slocum found himself playing the role of teacher. How to ride most of the day away without wearing out your ass or your horse. How to make a camp. How to cook a decent meal in a camp. How to break camp and clean up after yourself. How to take a little side trip and hunt for fresh meat along the way. How to clean it, butcher it and cook it. How to boil up a good pot of coffee. And Golden paid attention all right. He was learning. Slocum figured the kid would turn out all right.

"Slocum," asked Golden, as they rode along easy, "when we get there, how will I find my place?"

"The first thing we'll do," Slocum said, "is look up that lawyer who wrote you the letter."

"Grimes," Golden said.

"Yeah," said Slocum. "Whatever. We'll track him down, and he oughta be able to give us the whole lowdown on the place. Where to find it. Whether it's up and running. All that stuff. He'll have some papers for you to sign. I'm sure of that. They always do."

"What kind of papers?"

"Oh, papers registering the place in your name. That kind of thing."

"Oh."

They rode a ways in silence. Slocum took a cigar out of his pocket and fired it up with a wooden match. It was a still day, and the smoke drifted up and back as they moved along the road.

"I just can't hardly get used to the idea of me being a man of property," Golden said. "It don't hardly seem real."

"You'll get used to it soon enough," Slocum said. "Once you find out how much work it is trying to hold the place together, paying your hands and all your bills. Keeping your cows fat and watching the price of beef. You'll get used to it all right. You might even decide that it's too much to worry with. Might decide to sell the place."

"No," said Golden. "I won't do that. I got me something in this life now. I ain't never had nothing before. Not nothing. I mean to hang onto this ranch. It's mine. I won't sell it. No, sir. Not for nothing."

Slocum shrugged.

"I hope it turns out to be everything you want in a place," he said.

"I know it will be," said Golden. "I just know it. I got me a feeling about it already."

When the sun was low in the western sky, Slocum scouted out a good campsite. It was underneath a clump of willows that grew along the bank of a clear running creek. There was grass for the horses, wood for a fire, water for drinking, cooking and washing. Golden got busy setting up the camp. He was used to the routine by this time. In a short while a small fire was burning and coffee was boiling in the pot.

"I guess we can stand to eat just trail food tonight," Slocum said, "being as how this will be our last camp."

"Last camp?" asked Golden. "You mean—"

"I figure we'll come onto Harleyville tomorrow before noon, so we'll have us a breakfast here in the morning, but we'll find someone else to cook for us by noon. Then we'll hunt up that lawyer and then ride out to take a look at your ranch."

"Hot damn. I can't hardly wait. Wonder if I got a cook out at the place?"

"Well," Slocum said, "if you've got a crew, you'll have a cook. Crew has to eat."

"I hope he's a good one. Say, Slocum, how about we get us a bottle of good whiskey in Harleyville, and then take it with us out to the ranch so you and me can celebrate. We'll get good and drunk. I don't mean to do that just any old night, you know, but it seems to me like tomorrow will be a day that ought to be celebrated right proper. What do you say?"

"Let's wait till we see what it is you got to celebrate, ole pard," Slocum said. "Then if it's what you think it's going to be, we'll tie one on all right."

Breakfast in the morning was hard biscuits and bacon with coffee. Golden had been up well before Slocum, and he would have preferred to slurp down a cup of coffee and hit the road, he was so anxious to get to his ranch. But Slocum insisted on taking the time for some food, and he lingered over several cups of coffee. Finally he figured that he had tormented young Golden long enough, so he started packing things up. Golden cleaned up the campsite in a hurry. At last they were ready to ride, and when they mounted up and started on their way, Slocum had to slow Golden down.

"You won't see that place any sooner if you wear your horse out along the way," he said.

Slocum had been right. The sun was high overhead when they spotted Harleyville ahead. It was a small town, but not too small. Most of the town's buildings were lined up on the two sides of one long street. As they rode in, they could see that Harleyville had a church, a saloon, a general store, a couple of eateries, a schoolhouse, a stable, a hotel, a blacksmith's shop, two law offices, a sheriff's office and jail combined and other miscellaneous businesses. Slocum pulled up in front of the first of the two eating places they came to. As he dismounted, Golden rode up beside him.

"Hey," he said, "let's go see Mr. Grimes."

"We'll eat first," Slocum said.

Golden wanted to argue, but he had ridden with Slocum long enough to know better. If he had argued, he knew, Slocum would just have told him to go on and do what he wanted to do. He did not want to do it without Slocum along. So, anxious as he was, he tied his horse to the rail there beside the big Appaloosa and went inside with Slocum. The place was busy. There were only a couple of available tables.

"Maybe the other place ain't so busy," Golden said.

"It'll be the same way," said Slocum. "Didn't you notice how crowded the town is? There's something going on here today to draw in so many people. It's the noon hour too, so both eating places will be like this. Let's grab us that table over yonder."

It took a little while for them to get service, but when they did, they had steak and potatoes and biscuits and gravy. They washed it all down with plenty of coffee. Since they had arrived late, by the time they finished their meals most of the other customers had already left the place. The waiter came back to pour more coffee.

"Say," Slocum asked, "is Harleyville always this busy?"

"No," said the waiter. "It's usually pretty calm."

"What's going on?" Slocum asked.

"Oh, there's a big important hearing over at the saloon," the man said. "The judge is in town, and everyone's come to town to hear what he'll have to say."

"Some kind of criminal case?" Slocum asked.

"Nope. Civil," the man said, and he turned and walked away before Slocum could quiz him further.

"What's that mean?" Golden asked. "That civil?"

"Well, it means that it ain't criminal," said Slocum.

"What goes to court that ain't criminal?"

"Oh, someone sues someone else over something," Slocum said.

"You about done yet?"

"I'm going to finish off this last cup of coffee," said Slocum. "Stop fidgeting. It occurs to me that with some civil matter that drawed in this many folks, every lawyer in the country's going to be in that hearing. We won't find your Grimes in his office. Not now."

"Aw, shit," Golden said. "Hell. Well, I think we oughta go try anyhow. You could be wrong about that. Maybe he ain't involved. Maybe it's that other lawyer feller in town."

"I'll bet you your boots that they're both in that hearing," Slocum said. He polished off his coffee and stood up. "Let's go," he said.

Just to humor Golden, Slocum walked with him to Grimes's office. They found the door locked.

"Damn it," said Golden.

"Come on," Slocum said.

They walked to the saloon, but the place was packed, and people were hanging around the doorway trying to hear what was being said inside. Slocum spotted a man who was back far enough that he couldn't possibly hear what was going on in there. He walked over to the man.

"Howdy," he said.

"Howdy yourself, stranger," the man said.

"My name's Slocum. I just rode into town. Can you tell me what's going on here?"

"Stout's mine," the man said, extending his hand. Slocum shook it. "Judge is handing down his big decision."

"Decision on what?"

"The land grant claim," said Stout.

"Well, say, is the lawyer Grimes in there?"

"Sure. He's the man representing all the ranchers with Whistling Valley spreads. He's in there all right."

Slocum thought a minute about what Stout had said. Grimes was inside representing the ranchers with Whistling Valley ranches in a hearing that has something to do with a land grant claim. It sounded fishy to him. He wanted to quiz the man further, but something stopped him. He could wait till the hearing was over and then catch up with Grimes. He could wait, but he wasn't sure that Golden could.

2

All of a sudden, the crowd started coming out of the saloon. Men were grumbling. Women were crying. Anger and desolation both showed equally in their faces. Slocum watched with interest, and Golden watched with anxious curiosity.

"No one's moving me off my place," one man said.

"You heard Potter," said another. "He'll arrest any man what don't obey the law."

"He'll have to come with his guns out."

"What's going on, Slocum?" Golden asked. "What happened in there?"

"I don't know any more than you do, kid," Slocum said. "Just hold your horses and we'll find out in good time."

They waited and watched and listened as the people kept coming out of the saloon, the temporary courthouse, grousing and grumbling. Some climbed into wagons, others mounted horses. Slowly the crowd dispersed. Some hung around town in small clusters bellyaching together or strategizing. When the place had cleared out enough, Slocum gestured at Golden.

"Let's go inside," he said.

With court over, the saloon had reopened. A number of men had bellied up to the bar. Slocum and Golden did the same and waited their turn. When the bartender finally got around to them, they each ordered a shot of whiskey. Slocum noticed a man in a three-piece suit seated at a table with three cowhand-looking fellows. They seemed to be in deep and serious conversation. It was obvious that something big had happened in this room just a few minutes ago, and it had had something to do with that land grant they had heard rumblings about. The land grant and the properties in an area known as Whistling Valley. Well, sooner or later, they would find Grimes back in his office, and then they would get it all cleared up.

Slocum hailed the barkeep and ordered two more drinks. He thought again, paid for the bottle and took it up and led Golden to an empty table.

"This ain't exactly where and how you meant to get drunk tonight," he said, "but it might have to do till we find out what's going on around here."

"Shit, I reckon," said Golden.

"You know, we might oughta get us a hotel room and stable our horses," Slocum said. "The way things look, we might not even catch up with that Grimes today."

"This sure ain't what I was looking forward to," said Golden.

Slocum looked around the room. It seemed cold and unfriendly. He downed the whiskey in his glass and stood up, taking the bottle by the neck.

"Let's get out of here," he said.

They walked out of the saloon and across the street to the hotel, where they got themselves a room. Then, without going up to it, they went out again and back across the street to their horses. Mounting up, they rode to the stable and put the animals up for the night. Walking back toward the hotel, Slocum noticed the man in the three-piece suit from the saloon walking along the street. He stopped.

"What is it?" Golden asked.

"Just wait up a minute," said Slocum.

As he watched, the three-piece-suited man went to the door of the Grimes law office, pulled a key out of his pocket, unlocked the door and went inside.

"That's him," Slocum said. "Let's go."

As they stepped into the office, Grimes looked up from behind his desk.

"Yes?" he said. "What can I do for you?"

"I'm Sammy Golden," said Golden, holding out the letter Grimes had written to him regarding his inheritance. Grimes took the letter and glanced at it briefly before handing it back. "This is my friend John Slocum."

Grimes offered his hand to the two men and they shook.

"Sit down," he said. He sat again behind his desk. "I don't know how much you men managed to take in regarding what just happened here today, but I'm afraid that I have some distressing news, at least for the time being."

"What is it?" Golden asked.

"Well," said Grimes, "it was only a day or so after I sent your letter. A man named Smoot showed up in town with an old land grant. He claimed that it gave him title to all of Whistling Valley. I'm afraid that includes your property, Mr. Golden. There are a number of ranches in that valley. A lot of people are upset."

"We could see that much for ourselves," Slocum said.

"You mean, he's just taking over, just like that?" Golden asked. "I ain't got no ranch after all?"

"Not exactly," Grimes said. "Of course, his grant was challenged for authenticity. The ranchers came to me for help. That's why the hearing today. The judge came in from the territorial capital to hear the case. He examined all the documents, and today he ruled that the land grant is authentic and valid. Smoot owns all of Whistling Valley. He says he wants everyone to pack up and get out or else start paying him rent.

"Now, according to the judge, Smoot has every right to make those demands. I'm not quitting though. I'm appealing his decision and looking further into the validity of that so-called land grant of his. In the meantime, according to the law, you and all the other Whistling Valley ranch owners have to pay him rent or get out."

"Well," Golden said, "at least I don't have to move out. Hell. I've never moved in. Say, can I at least take a look at the place that was supposed to be mine?"

"I don't see why not," said Grimes. "I'll give you directions to the place."

*   *   *

Grimes gave them directions and told them that it was about a two-hour ride out to the place. He also told them that Smoot had set up his own headquarters out there. As anxious as Golden was to take a look at what might have been his ranch, Slocum suggested that, as late in the afternoon as it was, the ride out and back was too long.

"Let's ride out in the morning," he said. "Right after breakfast."

Reluctantly, Golden agreed.

They decided to try the other eatery for supper. After their meal, they agreed that one was about as good as the other, or bad, as the case may be. Slocum was still carrying the whiskey bottle around by its neck, so they decided to go back to the saloon for a place to sit and drink. Perhaps the mood would have changed by then. They walked over to it and went inside, finding themselves a table. The place was almost empty, but there were four cowboys bellied up to the bar.

"Son of a bitch ain't going to run me off my place," Slocum heard one of them say.

"Calm down, Dave," said another. "Grimes is looking into the whole deal."

"Lawyers can look into things for years," said the one called Dave. "And what am I supposed to do while he's a looking? Pay that bastard five hundred dollars a month to stay on my own place? Hell, I ain't got that kind of money. I'll be dead broke in three months. Shit no, Lefty. Anyone comes onto my place meaning to move me out or collect rent better come a-shooting."

"Can't say I blame you," Lefty said, "but I don't know. I wouldn't want Potter coming after me with a posse."

"Fuck Potter."

"Aw, say, he's just doing his job is all, and he don't like it none either."

"I'd quit a job before I'd put honest folks offa their own property."

Sammy Golden stood up and started to move toward the bar. Slocum reached out and put a hand on his arm.

"Careful, boy," he said.

"Ah, I ain't looking for no trouble, Slocum," Golden said.

He walked on over to the bar to stand beside Dave. "Excuse me," he said, "I don't mean to butt in, and I didn't mean to be eavesdropping neither, but I couldn't help overhearing some of what you was saying. My name's Sammy Golden, and I just got in town. I inherited me a ranch in Whistling Valley. At least, I thought I did till I got here and found out what's going on."

"What spread you inherit?" Dave asked.

Golden took out his letter from Grimes and handed it to Dave. As Dave was reading, Golden said, "Grimes called it the Box Spring."

"You know the place, Dave," Lefty said.

"Yeah, I know it. It's a nice place. Only thing is, Smoot and his bunch have moved in on it."

"That's what Grimes said."

"It was the only place in the valley what didn't have a owner on it," Lefty said, "so whenever Smoot come along the whole crew just packed up and left. Smoot moved on in."

"So what do you mean to do?" Dave asked.

"I don't know," Golden said. "I hadn't even got used to the idea of owning a ranch yet. Then I come into town and found out that I maybe don't own it after all. I ain't had time to figure things out."

"Seems to me there ain't nothing to figure on," Dave said. "You own that piece of property, same as I own my place. Now this bastard Smoot is claiming that he owns ever' damn thing in the valley. I say we all get together and fight them off—Smoot, the sheriff, anyone who tries to put us off our own land."

"What the hell do you think would happen, Dave," said Lefty, "if you or any one of the boys was to shoot the sheriff or any of his deputies? You think that'd be the end of it? It ain't likely. Why, there'd be U.S. marshals in here before you could wipe your ass. Maybe even the U.S. Army."

"I'll fight them too if they try to put me off my own place. I'll fight and die before I'll just up and walk away from what I know is mine."

Golden, still perplexed, looked toward where Slocum still sat at the table, drinking alone.

"Slocum," he said, "you hearing any of this?"

"Ever' word," Slocum said. "You all ain't exactly whispering."

"I don't give a damn who hears me," said Dave. "I'll say it to the sheriff, to Smoot, to the U.S. marshals and the damned cavalry."

"What do you make of it all, Slocum?" Golden asked.

"I can't say," Slocum said. "Both men are right in what they say. There ain't no right answer in a situation like this. That's how come I stay footloose. I don't get these kinds of worries."

Golden moved back to the table and sat in a chair directly opposite Slocum. He leaned in toward Slocum, a serious expression on his face.

"But, Slocum," he said, "if it was your place—"

"Wouldn't be my place."

"Hell, you never know. I never bought the place. I didn't work for it the way Dave here worked for his. I just got a damn letter in the mail, that's all. Before I got that letter, I'd a said the same as you. I'd a said it couldn't never happen to me. But it did. So what if it had happened to you 'stead of me? What would you do?"

"Sammy, I ain't in that position. I don't know what I'd do."

Golden, exasperated, looked back toward Dave and Lefty.

"You two fellas want to join us here?" he asked.

Dave picked up his glass and headed for the table, and Lefty followed.

"Don't mind if we do," Dave said. He and Lefty took chairs at the table.

"Dave and Lefty," Golden said, "this here is my friend John Slocum."

They howdied around the table, and then Dave said, "Slocum, I'll ask you a question, if you don't mind."

Slocum shrugged.

"You say you're footloose. Free as a bird. I reckon you own a horse."

"I do."

"All right then. Suppose a man come up to you with a piece of paper and the sheriff alongside him to back it up, and he says to you that's his horse, and the paper proves it. You going to just hand him the reins?"

"I've killed more than one man who tried to steal my horse," Slocum said.

"But this one's got a paper and he's got the sheriff."

"Would you hand him the reins?" Golden asked.

"All right, Dave," said Slocum. "You made your point. But let's think this thing out real careful. Let me see if I got everything lined up right. This Smoot, he's got a paper that says he owns the whole valley. The judge studied the paper and says that Smoot is right. He owns it all. But Lawyer Grimes don't agree. He's fixing to take it on up the line in the court system. Am I right?"

"That's right," Lefty said.

"Then before you go off half-cocked and maybe get someone killed, maybe even yourself, why don't you give ole Grimes a chance? Maybe he's right, and maybe he can prove it."

"Because it's going to take time, Slocum," said Dave. "And the judge has give Smoot the land already. Smoot says we got to move off or pay rent, and if we don't, the sheriff's going to come out to run us off. That's what's going to be happening if we just sit back and wait for Grimes."

"Pay the rent till Grimes gets that decision made proper," Slocum said.

"Two months, three at the outside," Dave said, "I'd be broke. So would most all the rest of the ranchers in the valley."

"Where's this Smoot hang out?" Slocum asked.

Lefty laughed out loud, and he and Dave both looked at Golden.

"He's set up his headquarters right out there at your pard's place, like you said," Dave answered.

"You mean, he stays out there all the time? He's got no place in town?"

"He's living out there in the ranch house."

"Has he got a crew?" Slocum asked.

"He's got a bunch of men out there that he calls cowhands," Dave said. "I think they're a bunch of gunfighters and toughs."

"I can't see no cow work going on out there," Lefty said.

Grimes walked in the door just then. He was headed for the bar, but when he saw the table full of his clients, he veered over that way.

"Good evening, gentlemen," he said. "It's been a long day."

"Sit down and have a drink with us?" Golden asked.

"Thanks," said Grimes. "I can use it."

Golden jumped up, went to the bar and got another glass. He brought it to the table, poured it full of whiskey and shoved the glass in front of the attorney.

"Boys," he said, "I don't know what you've been talking about, don't know what you're planning, but I've got something to tell you. I'm leaving for the capital in the morning. It'll take me about two weeks to go over there, get my business taken care of, and get back here. If you can manage it, don't do anything until I get back. Just hold out. That's all."

"What's up?" asked Dave.

"I mean to file a paper that will put a legal stop to everything Smoot is doing until the case can be heard in a higher court."

"Can you do that?"

"Simplest thing in the world," said Grimes. "It's just a matter of going all the way to the capital to get it done. That's all."

Slocum gave the eye to Dave.

"Well, now," Dave said, "that does put a new face on things. Maybe we can hold out for two weeks."

"It's worth a try," Lefty said.

"It's no problem for me," said Golden. "Hell, I ain't been living on my place anyhow. Ain't even seen it yet."

"Would you boys do me a big favor?" asked Grimes.

"What's that?"

"Spread the word to the rest of the ranchers. Tell them what I'm doing. Ask them to hold off too. Two weeks. That's all I'm asking."

"We'll get on it first thing in the morning," Dave said.

"Thanks," said Grimes. He drained his glass and stood up. "And thanks for the drink."

"You don't have to rush off," said Golden.

"I'm afraid I do," said Grimes. "I have to get everything together for my trip tomorrow. The stage leaves early."

As Grimes walked out the door, Golden was refilling glasses around the table.

"That man's working hard for us," said Lefty. "He's a good man."

"About two weeks," Dave said. "We'll see in two weeks how good he is."

"Even if gets that paper filed," said Slocum, "that's just the first step. Like he said, that just holds Smoot off till the things gets back in court. Ain't no guarantee what that court decision will finally be."

"It gives us some time though," Dave said. "Say, where you two staying?"

"We got us a room over at the hotel," Golden said.

"You done paid for the night?"

"Yeah."

"Well, you might as well get what you paid for, but in the morning, why don't you pack up and come on out to my place? Be my guests."

Golden looked at Slocum.

"Well, I—"

"That's mighty kind of you," Slocum said. "How do we find you?"

"You know where his place is?" Dave asked, jerking a thumb at Golden.

"Grimes gave us directions," said Slocum.

"When you get to it just keep on riding to the next gate. That'll be me. My spread's called the Ringy Dingy."

"We'll see you then," Slocum said.

"Thanks," said Golden. "That's mighty good of you."

"Hey," said Dave, "we're all in this son of a bitch together. Well, good night. I'm headed for the house. You coming along, Lefty?"

"I reckon so."

Alone at the table, Slocum and Golden decided to have one last drink before heading over to the hotel.

"Slocum," said Golden, "I got you down here in the middle of a mess. You said the reason you won't settle down is that you don't have to worry with such things. Well, if you want to ride on out, I won't think no less of you."

"I try not to get myself in the middle of a mess," Slocum said, "but I have another rule. I don't run out on friends."

3

John Slocum and Sammy Golden pulled up in front of the big gate that was the entrance to the place Golden had inherited and then lost, both so unexpectedly. There was no sign over the gate, or anywhere else for that matter, no name, not even a brand. They knew they were at the right place, though, because of the directions and the description given to them by Grimes.

"What do you think, Slocum?" asked Golden.

"From here, it looks pretty good," Slocum said. " 'Course, it don't look too active."

"There's some horses down there by the big house," said Golden.

"I see them."

"You reckon that Smoot is down there?"

Slocum shrugged.

"We never seen him in town," he said. "Grimes and ole Dave both told us that he was staying out here."

"Let's go on down there and meet him," said Golden. "Maybe he'll let us ride over the place."

"What good's that going to do?"

"Maybe none," said Golden, "but I'd like to get a closer look. That's all."

"Suit yourself," Slocum said.

They turned their horses to ride down the lane that led to the big house. It was two stories, and a big porch ran the width of the front wall. The porch was covered and the roof formed a second story porch. As they drew close to the house, two men stepped out onto the porch. Within a few feet of the porch, Slocum and Golden hauled up.

"Howdy," Golden said.

"You got business here?" one of the men on the porch asked.

"I'd like to see Mr. Smoot," Golden said.

"And who are you?"

"Sam Golden. This is John Slocum with me."

The man who had challenged Golden glanced over at his partner. The other man turned toward the door.

"I'll see," he said, and he disappeared into the house. They waited for a long and anxious moment. At last a third man stepped out onto the porch, followed by the one who had just gone in. The newcomer, dressed in a black, three-piece suit, wearing a black hat and sporting a handlebar mustache, stepped to the edge of the porch and looked at the two visitors.

"I'm Smoot," he said. "What can I do for you?"

"I'm Sam Golden. I just got to town and found out what's going on here. You see, I got a letter saying that I'd inherited this place."

"Oh, yeah. Golden. I remember now," Smoot said. "Well, if you found out what's going on, you know that it ain't your place. It's mine, along with the rest of this valley."

"I didn't come here to argue about that," said Golden. "I just wanted to ask you if it might be all right if me and Slocum here was to ride over the place. Kind of see what I almost had."

"I don't think that'd be a good idea, Golden," said Smoot. "You see, I've got hands out around the spread. In view of some of the talk that's been going on, they might be inclined to shoot first and ask questions later—if at all."

"I see. Well, the other thing I wanted to ask you was that I heard that you had offered to rent to the owners, uh, previous owners, if they wanted to stay on. Would you rent this place to me?"

"You can see that I've already set myself up here," Smoot said. "I made that offer to the others on account a I didn't want to throw folks out of their homes. I moved in here 'cause it was empty. If I was you, I'd just keep on riding. There ain't nothing for you here."

They rode silently for a space, on toward Dave's spread. Now and then, Golden turned in the saddle to look back toward what had almost been his own ranch.

"Of all the ranch owners in the valley," he said, "I guess I'm the only one that don't get to rent his own place, even if I was of a mind to pay the rent."

"I've got a feeling that you wouldn't a been able to afford his price anyhow," Slocum said. "He's going to asking way too much rent. He don't really want to set back and collect rent. He wants to run everyone out of the valley. That's the way it looks to me."

"You think so?"

"He may be set up back there at your place," Slocum said, "but he ain't set up to do no ranching. He says he got himself a crew out and around, but from what I've seen, it ain't a crew of cowhands. There's something going on around here more than what's out front and in the open."

"Well, what is it?"

"Don't know, but it's something. Here's ole Dave's place. Let's ride on in."

A sign over the gate read Ringy Dingy Ranch. There was no mistaking that. They rode under the gate sign and headed for the ranch house. A white-haired man was standing on the porch. As they drew close, he hailed them.

"Welcome," he said. "You the boys Dave invited out?"

Golden dismounted and walked to the porch, his hand extended.

"Yes, sir," he said. "I'm Sam Golden."

"I'm Carlton Bradley," the man said, shaking Golden's hand. "I'm Dave's old man."

"It's a pleasure, Mr. Bradley," Golden said. "This here is John Slocum."

Slocum had by that time dismounted and walked over to the porch. He shook hands with Bradley.

"Glad to know you, Mr. Bradley," he said. "Say, is this all right with you?"

"Sure it is," Bradley said. "Besides, I pretty well turned the place over to Dave a few years ago. I'm getting too old for most of the work around here. Oh, I do a little every now and then, but mostly, I let Dave run it."

Just then a cowboy rounded the corner of the house. Bradley waved him over.

"Milt," he said, "meet John Slocum and Sam Golden. Dave invited them out to stay a spell with us."

"Glad to meet you," Milt said, shaking hands with them.

"Why don't you take care of their horses, Milt?" Bradley said.

"Sure thing."

As Milt took up the reins of the two horses, Bradley turned back to Slocum and Golden.

"Come on in the house, boys," he said. "Dave'll be glad to see you."

They had just stepped inside when Dave saw them and came hurrying across the room to shake their hands and bid them welcome to the Ringy Dingy Ranch. In another moment a young woman stepped into the room from the kitchen.

"Hey, Sis, come over here," Dave said. "I want you to meet a couple of new friends. This is Sammy Golden, and this here is John Slocum. Boys, my sister, Julie."

Her hair was yellow with just a hint of red, and her eyes were blue, not watery blue, but a deep, bright blue. She was small in stature, but well filled out, and she was dressed like a boy, with her shirttail tucked into her tight-fitting jeans. She smiled when she took Golden's hand and looked into his eyes.

"I'm glad to meet you, Sammy," she said. "Dave tells us that you're our new next-door neighbor."

"Well," said Golden, doffing his hat, "I guess that all depends on how all this business works out."

"It'll work out," said Dave, "and you'll be sitting in that ranch house instead of that bastard Smoot."

"Either that or we'll all be six feet under," said old Bradley. Slocum saw that Dave had got his stubbornness honestly, inherited from his father.

Julie slipped her hand out of Golden's and turned to Slocum.

"Mr. Slocum," she said, "welcome to our home."

"Thank you, ma'am," he said. "It's a pleasure to make your acquaintance."

"Well, I'd better be getting back to the kitchen," she said, "or there won't be any lunch when the time comes. You two will join us right in here."

Golden stared after her as she moved across the room and through the door back into the kitchen. He was smitten. She was beautiful, a vision of loveliness the likes of which he had never seen before. Slocum could see it in Golden's face. He thought about taking the young man aside and cautioning him to remember that they were guests in this house. Then he thought, what the hell? They're both young. Mind your own business. Let nature take its course. If things got hot over the issue, then Slocum could always just ride away. He had no stake in this valley.

"Well," Bradley said, "don't just stand around. Find yourselves a seat."

The four men got seated in the large and comfortable living room, and Bradley took a cigar out of his pocket and lit it. He held up a box and offered them around. Dave and Golden each declined the offer, but Slocum accepted gladly.

"What did you think of your place?" Dave asked Golden.

Golden shook his head.

"Didn't hardly seem like mine with that Smoot and his gang over there," he said. "We rode up to the house to meet Smoot. He come out all right. Wouldn't let us ride around to look the place over, and he said that he won't rent it to me. He's living there. He told us to hit the road. Go on someplace else. Ain't nothing here for me. That's what he said."

"Before this is over," Bradley said, "he's going to find out there's nothing here for him but a hole six feet deep. I've got half a mind to get the boys together right now and ride over there. Hell, we could wipe that bunch out before anyone knew anything was going on."

"That's how I feel too, Dad," Dave said, "but last night ole Grimes said that he was going to the capital today to file some kinda papers that would put a stop to Smoot till we can get the thing back in court again. He asked me to spread the word. He wants us all to wait and give him a chance to work it all out legal."

"Well, we might give him a few days," Bradley said.

"He said the trip would take him two weeks," said Golden.

"What do you say, Slocum?" Bradley asked.

"It ain't none of my business, Mr. Bradley," Slocum said. "I'm just riding along with Sammy here, temporarily. You have your home in this valley. When this is all over and done with, whatever the outcome, I'll be back riding the trail to nowhere."

"Maybe that's why I want to know what you think. You're not as wrapped up in it as we are. Maybe you can see more clearly from where you stand."

"Has anyone come around yet to either collect rent or tell you to get out?"

"Not yet."

"Then I'd say don't do nothing till that happens. When someone does come around to pay the rent, could you pay it?"

"Pay rent to live on my own ranch," Bradley said. "Why, I'd die fighting first. I'd—"

Slocum spread his hands in a gesture of futility.

"I said it was none of my business," he said.

Bradley sucked in a deep breath.

"I'm sorry," he said. "I did press you. All right. I ain't saying I would, but, yes, I could pay it."

"Then I'd say pay it," Slocum said. "That'll keep things quiet for a month. In just two weeks, Grimes will be back with the word on what happened at the capital. Chances are, Smoot'll have to return the rent he collected, move out of Sammy's house and wait it out till court time."

"That does make a kind of sense," Bradley admitted grudgingly. "It makes sense for those like us, but there's some that won't be able to pay, and there's some others that'll be hurting for cash if they pay up."

"Maybe something can be done about that," Slocum said.

"I got just enough that I could pay one month's rent,"

Golden said. "But ole Smoot, he won't take it from me. I could maybe help out someone who can't pay."

"That's mighty big of you," Bradley said. "What do you say, son?"

"I reckon Slocum's right," Dave said. "Let's wait till they contact us, and if all they do is ask for rent, let's go on and pay it. It'll just be the one time."

"Then it's decided," Bradley said. "Now, Dave, you told me that Grimes wants us to ride around and spread the word."

"That's right."

"Then let's get on it right after lunch."

"I'll tell Lefty to take over here for the afternoon," Dave said.

"Lefty?" said Golden.

"Yeah," said Dave. "You met him last night. Lefty's our foreman."

"Oh?"

"I'll ride along with you, if that's all right," Slocum said.

"You'll be welcome," said Bradley.

"Me too," said Golden. "I'd like to get some idea of the lay of the land and meet some of the folks. They might wind up being my neighbors."

"Ain't no might about it," Bradley said. "They will be your neighbors."

They had stopped at two places and convinced the owners to go along with the plan. The next place along the road, Bradley told them, belonged to a widow woman named Sally Clay. She had not had it easy since losing her husband two years ago. Rance Clay had been a good friend of Bradley's, and Bradley had done what he could to help Sally keep her small place together. She had a couple of cowhands. That was all she could afford. She might be a tough sell.

"Say," said Golden. "Maybe she'd be the one I ought to use my money for."

"Maybe so," Bradley said. "Come on. Let's go have a talk with her."

They kicked up their mounts and rode on around a bend in the road to a small gate. The fence needed mending right there at the gate. It was obvious from the start that the place was in need of some serious work. They moved through the gate and on down the lane. It curved around a clump of trees to reveal the small house hidden there from passersby. Slocum noted that the roof was in need of repairs. They stopped their horses in front of the house. No one came out. They dismounted and tied their horses, and Bradley called out. There was no response.

"Wonder where she could be," he said.

Dave stepped to the front door and pounded on it. He waited a moment with no response. Then they heard the sound of approaching hoofbeats. They all looked in the direction of the sound. A short time later, a woman came riding up from around the house. Slocum took in her appearance at once. She was somewhere between thirty-five and forty, he thought, and she showed signs of hard work. Even so, she was still a damn good-looking woman. He was a bit surprised, probably because Bradley had said that her husband had been a good friend of his. He had expected someone closer to Bradley's age.

"Sally," Bradley said. "Is everything all right here?"

"Hell, no," she said. "After all that bullshit in town from that son-of-a-bitch Smoot, my boys up and quit on me. I been out checking on some new calves. I got to do it all now."

She dismounted and walked over to take Bradley's hand.

"I'm sorry to hear that," Bradley said. "Sally, I want you to meet John Slocum and Sam Golden."

"Howdy, boys," said Sally. "Sorry I give you such a rough welcome."

"We understand, Miz Clay," Slocum said.

"Come on in the house," she said. "I'll heat up some coffee."

"Sally," Bradley said, "we got a plan of action we hope you'll go along with. And I want to ask you to just keep quiet till you've heard it all. I interrupted Slocum a time or two while he was laying it out to me, and I shouldn't have."

"I'll listen," Sally said. They were seated around a table in Sally's small house, each with a cup of steaming coffee.

"Okay, then, here's the deal," said Bradley. He hesitated. "Oh, hell, Slocum, you can say it all better than I can. You tell her."

"Well, it's simple," Slocum said. "Grimes has gone to the capital to file papers that will stop Smoot till the deal gets back in court. He'll be gone for two weeks, and the way I see it, that two weeks is all you ranch owners have to worry about. So I suggested that you all pay Smoot one month's rent and then just wait for Grimes to do the rest."

"That's it?"

"Yes, ma'am."

"What if Grimes loses in court when we get back in there?"

"Mr. Bradley and some of the others have been talking about fighting," Slocum said. "If you lose the case in court, I reckon that'll be time enough to fight."

"Well, that might be good enough for the rest of you," she said, "but I couldn't pay fifty cents rent. It took everything I had to pay off those two cowboys when they quit on me. Ah, hell, I just as well give it all up and ride out of this damn valley for good."

"Where would you go, Sally?" Bradley said. "This is your home."

"I don't know what I'd do or where I'd go," she said. "I guess I could always go to some city and go to whoring for a living."

"God damn it, Sally," said Bradley, "I won't have you talking like that."

"Excuse me, Mr. Bradley," Golden said. "Do you think now I could . . ."

He hesitated, and Bradley finally caught on.

"Oh, yeah. Yeah. This is as good a time as any, Sam."

"Mrs. Clay," Golden said, "Smoot won't take my money. He's living on my place. I'd be proud to pay your month's rent for you. I expect we'll get the rent money back anyhow soon as Mr. Grimes wins the case."

Sally looked stunned.

"Take it, Sally," Bradley said.

"I don't reckon I'm needed over at the Bradley place," said Slocum. "If you'll let me put up in your bunkhouse and feed me a little, I'll help you work this place till everything's straightened out around here."

Sally still couldn't find words, so Dave, who had been quiet through all this, decided to find the right ones for her.

"Well, by God," he said. "I reckon that just about takes care of everything."

"We still have a few more ranches to visit," Bradley said, standing up, "so we'll be on our way."

"I'll finish out the day with them," Slocum said to Sally, "if that's all right. Then I'll pack up my stuff and ride over here first thing in the morning."

"Yeah," she said. "Sure. That'll be just fine. First thing in the morning."

4

"Well," Golden said, as the riders pulled up in front of the headquarters of the Ringy Dingy Ranch, "we only lost one."

They had spent the entire day riding over the valley, talking with the ranch owners, and all but old Zeb Price had agreed to try their best to stick out the two weeks and give Grimes a chance to win the case for them. It was already getting dark. A cowhand met them there in front of the porch and took the horses.

"Ole Price ain't much of a loss," Bradley said. "He's a worthless ole bastard, and he was going broke anyhow. He never had no business trying to run a ranch. But the rest is all sticking together, and that's good. Say, a day like today calls for a drink. Let's all go in and have one."

Just then Julie stepped out on the porch.

"How'd it go?" she asked.

"Everybody's sticking but just ole Price," Dave said.

"That's good," said Julie. "You want me to put on some coffee?"

"No," said Bradley. "We're fixing to have us a drink of whiskey. Come on in, boys."

As the other three found places to sit, Bradley got out the whiskey and glasses and poured a round. With everyone served, he sat in his favorite easy chair. Then he lifted his glass.

"To success," he said.

The others raised their glasses and repeated his toast. Julie came into the room.

"Is this a male meeting," she asked, "or is anyone welcome here?"

Golden jumped to his feet.

"Oh, please join us, ma'am," he said.

"Can I have a glass of that whiskey, Dad?" she said.

"Help yourself, darlin'," he said.

Golden walked over to the table containing the bottle and glasses. "Allow me," he said, and he poured Julie a drink and handed it to her.

"Thank you," she said. "It's nice to have a gentleman around the place for a change."

Golden blushed deep red and ducked his head. "Thank you, ma'am," he said.

"Call me Julie," she said. "And you're Sam. Right?"

"That's right, ma'am, uh, Julie."

"Well, Slocum," said Bradley in a booming voice, "you come up with this bright idea of paying a month's rent. What do we do next?"

"Just go on about your business," Slocum said. "Sooner or later Smoot's going to send someone around to collect the rent. When that happens, pay it. In two weeks ole Grimes'll be back, and we'll know whether or not he got his stay on Smoot."

"What if he ain't got it?"

"That'll be up to you. You said before you would fight for this land. If Grimes comes back without the stay, then maybe it will be time to fight. I don't know. It ain't my place to say one way or the other on that."

"We'll fight," Dave said. "We damn sure won't tuck our tails and just ride out of here."

"What about you, Golden?" Bradley asked.

"Well, I—I ain't made up my mind on that issue yet."

"It seems to me if you own a ranch and someone tries to steal it from you," said Junie, "you'd want to stand your ground and fight for what's yours."

"Well," Golden said, "if it comes to that, I'll fight."

Slocum gave Golden a sideways look. It was obvious to him that Golden's response, and his quick decision, was made especially for Julie Bradley. Amazing, he thought, how a young man's mind can be twisted and turned so easily by a good-looking young woman. Oh well, he had likely made some rash decisions himself on that same basis in his own misspent youth. The question now was what would Slocum do? If Grimes should fail, would Slocum stay and fight with Golden and the Bradleys and the rest? He was fast getting himself into this mess pretty deep. He turned up his glass and emptied it, and Bradley immediately offered him a refill. He accepted.

"It's a nice night out," Julie said. "I'd like to go out for a walk. Any of you brave men like to keep me company?"

The question was worded at all of the men, but Julie was looking right at Golden when she said it. He flushed again. He hesitated. After all, her father and brother were right there in the same room. He stood up, hat in hand, and glanced at old Bradley and at Dave.

"Well, I . . ."

"Go on, boy," said Bradley.

"Hey, she's a big girl," Dave said. "Hold her hand while you walk."

"Dave," Julie barked, but she offered her hand to Golden, and they walked out the front door together.

"I don't think you have to worry," Slocum said. "Ole Sammy's still wet behind the ears, and he's as polite as they come out here in these parts."

"Hell," Dave said, "it ain't Julie we're worried about. It's Sammy."

They strolled along hand in hand for a spell without talking. Golden was thrilled at the situation, but he was also embarrassed. He didn't know what to say, much less what to do. He was still thinking about her father and brother just inside the big house. Besides, he liked this young woman. He liked her very much, and he didn't want to do anything that might offend her. He told himself that if he made a move on her, she might find it too sudden and become angry at him. On the other hand, if he made no move whatsoever, she might take offense at that. He was thoroughly confused. At last he summoned up all his courage and spoke.

"You're right," he said. "It's a beautiful night."

"Yes, it is," she said. "Say, Sammy, back there when you said you'd stay and fight?"

"Yeah?"

"Did you say that just for me?"

Golden's face burned, and he was glad that it was dark out.

"Well," he said, "I—yeah. I guess I did."

"How come?"

"Aw, I don't know," he said. I just—well, I like you, Julie."

"So much that you'd make a decision to fight, maybe get yourself killed, on account of something I said?"

"Yeah. I guess so."

"You don't even know me," she said.

"Are you mad at me?" he asked. "I know I've only just met you, and for me to go saying that I like you and all, well—"

"I'm not mad," she said. She stopped walking and took hold of his shoulders, turning him to face her. She reached a hand behind his head, tilted it down, turned her own face up and kissed him on the lips. A tender kiss, not passionate, it promised more to come. Golden felt a thrill run throughout his body. She pulled herself loose, took his hand again and resumed their walk.

It was early the next morning when Slocum saddled his big Appaloosa and packed all his belongings either in the saddlebags or his blanket roll and mounted up to head for the small ranch of Sally Clay. The Bradleys and Golden would keep in close touch with him regarding any developments in the matter of Smoot's activities. In the meantime, he would help the widow Clay hold things together at her place. He meant to stick out the two weeks at least. After that, he wasn't sure. If Grimes got the stay, then everything ought to work out all right, and he could ride on. On the other hand, he had made this trip with Golden in order to help Golden get his own place set up and running. He might do that, hang around for a while. In the meantime, he could do more good helping the widow out than hanging around the Ringy Dingy. They had all the hands they needed.

Then there was the other possibility, the chance that Grimes would fail, and it would come to a fight. It was beginning to look as if Slocum would stick around for that if need be. The longer he stayed, the more he felt involved in the lives of these people, not just Golden, but the Bradleys and now the widow Clay. He guessed that he would likely be hanging around Whistling Valley for quite a spell.

The first thing Sally did was feed him a huge breakfast: eggs, biscuits, gravy, potatoes, ham. He had all he could eat, almost too much, and he washed it all down with cup after cup of good coffee. She was a fine cook, and, Slocum noted again, a fine-looking woman. When she offered him yet another cup of coffee, he held out his hand to stop her.

"I've had plenty," he said. "Thank you. And it was mighty good. Right now I think it's time for me to get to work. You got something you think needs doing before anything else?"

She shook her head.

"The place is so damn run down," she said, "I don't know where to start."

"In that case," he said, "I think I'll start with that fence out by your gate, if that's all right with you."

"That's fine," she said.

"After that," he said, "I'll just ride your fence line and check it all out. You, uh, you got wire and pliers and such?"

"Check in the barn," she said, "just to the left as you go in."

Slocum put on his hat and headed out the door.

"Slocum," she said.

He turned back to face her.

"Yes, ma'am?"

"I'm glad you're here. I appreciate it. And, say, call me Sally. Okay?"

Slocum smiled.

"Okay, Sally," he said. He touched the brim of his hat and turned to go out. Sally stood watching after him, even after he had closed the door. She stared at it as if she could still see him there. She had meant what she said to him. She was glad he was there. She sure could use the help. And he had the look of a man who would make a good hand. But she was glad to have him around for more reasons than that. It had been lonely for her on the ranch these last two years, and it was good to have someone else around for a change. It was good to have a man around. And this Slocum, well, he was a hell of a looking man, she told herself, and, though she had known him but a short time, she believed him to be a good man.

Just as Sally had said, Slocum found everything he needed in the barn. He had already, when he first arrived, turned the big Appaloosa into the corral and stowed his own gear in the small bunkhouse just beside the barn. He saddled up his horse again, gathered up what he thought he needed, and headed for the gate. He found that a couple of posts needed to be replaced and a few more needed to be snugged down. Then wire had to be stretched. It was noon before he had the job done. He rode back to the house and found that Sally had the noon meal all prepared. Again, he stuffed himself. If anything, it was better than the breakfast. He drank more coffee. Finished, he shoved his chair back.

"You sure are a fine cook, Sally," he said. "Thank you for that meal."

"You're more than welcome," she said. "It's the least I can do for you what with you coming over here to work for no pay."

"Well, so far," he said, "the two meals I've had are plenty of pay for the work I've done. Don't worry about that. I guess I better get back to it. I'd like to ride as much of that fence as I can today. Get on to something else tomorrow."

Riding the fence line, he found several places where he had to stop and tighten wire and a couple more places where fence posts needed straightening and snugging down. He was beginning to think that the rest of the job would be easy enough, when he came to a place where several feet of fence was completely down. There were cows on both sides of the fence. He rode slowly among them checking their brands, and he found two different brands. He had to go back to the barn anyhow, with so much fence down, so he decided to ask Sally about the brands at the same time.

He rode back to the house, and Sally, having heard his approach, stepped out the front door.

"I had to come back for some more supplies," he said. "There's a piece of fence clear down, and cows with two different brands are grazing on both sides. I thought I'd better check with you on the brands."

"You go on and get the supplies you need," she said. "I'll saddle up and ride back out there with you."

Back where the fence was down, Sally showed Slocum her brand. The other brand belonged to her neighbor just across the fence. Together, they rode among the cows, driving them back where they belonged. Some stubborn ones had to be chased back to Sally's land. With the two herds finally separated and back where they should be, Slocum started in on the fence. He figured that Sally would ride on back to the ranch house, but she did not. Instead, she dismounted and laid to right along side him. Slocum was impressed. She was as good as some men he had worked with.

They patched up the fence, mounted up and continued riding the line. By the time the sun was low in the western sky, they had almost reached the ranch house again. They had not come across any more problem areas in the fence.

"Slocum," she said, "that job's needed doing for a long time now, and I just hadn't been able to get to it. It sure feels better to have it all done."

"I'm glad to be of help," he said.

"Let's put the horses up and call it a day," she said. "I'll whomp you up a good supper."

Over at the Ringy Dingy, Golden was out riding the range with Lefty. Lefty was just looking the herd over, making sure that everything was okay. Golden had asked if he could ride along. He had gotten himself acquainted with the valley the day before riding out to visit all the ranchers, but he had not yet been very far off the road. Left had been pleased to have his company. They stopped on a rise and looked down on a grazing herd.

"Pretty good-looking cows," Golden said.

"Most folks in the valley have done pretty well this year," Lefty said. "If they can hold out for another month or so, it'll be time to drive them to market. Then even them that's broke will come out all right. It's been a good year. Cows are fat, and the price of beef is up. Everyone around here would be in great shape if it weren't for that damn Smoot."

Golden shook his head.

"Where does a son of a bitch like that come from?" he wondered.

"Out from under a rock," Lefty said, "or a pile of cow shit. Hey. Come on. I got something to show you."

Golden followed Lefty's lead on down into the low pasture and right through the grazing herd. Cattle lowed and scattered as the two riders invaded their previously contented lives. They rode another mile or so, and they came to a fence line. Cattle grazed on the other side of the fence. Lefty gestured over there.

"You know what that is?" he asked.

"Well, no," said Golden. "I can't say I do."

"That's your place over there, and I think I'd have to say that them are your cows too."

"Well, I'll be God damned," said Golden.

In the living room of Sammy Golden's ranch house, Smoot was meeting with two of his hired toughs. He sat behind a big desk, puffing a cigar. The two gunmen sat in chairs across the desk. Smoot had poured them each a glass of whiskey.

"You two are the rent collectors," he said. "I want you to ride the whole valley tomorrow. Stop at every ranch. The rent is two hundred dollars each for a month. Keep a record of everyone you collect from. If you don't find no one at home, make a note of it and go back later. If anyone refuses to pay you, make a note of that. I'll go see the sheriff and have him serve a notice on them. They might ask you to write them out a receipt. If they do, go on ahead and give it to them. If they ain't smart enough to ask, don't bother."

"You mean, if someone won't pay up, we just ride on off and leave them be?"

"The sheriff will take care of it for us," Smoot said. "We

don't need to get involved in no rough stuff. I mean that too. No rough stuff. Not just yet anyhow."

"Okay. You're the boss."

"I want you to start out with the Widda Clay," Smoot said. "The small ones and the ones who are the brokest will be the first ones to break. When we get rid of them, we can concentrate all our efforts on the tougher ones like Bradley."

"Okay."

"Now send in Art and Ned. I got a job for them two."

The two toughs downed what was left of their whiskey and went outside. A moment later, two more came in and sat down.

"You want us?" one said.

"That's right," said Smoot. "I got a job for you. Starting tomorrow night, and starting with the Widda Clay. I want you to ride out after dark and start in driving off her cattle. Herd them onto this place out into the far north pasture. Won't no one come in here snooping. These folks are trying to hold off, hoping that damn Grimes will do something for them, and if they can hold off till market time, they'll make some money. I want to break their backs before that time. If they lose enough cows, they'll give it up. They'll have to. Start in tomorrow night, and start with the Clay place."

"You got it, Boss."

5

They saw the two riders coming toward the house. Slocum pulled out his Colt and stepped into the next room, leaving the door open just a crack. It would be best, he thought, if Smoot's bunch did not know he was there with Sally Clay, at least for a while. At the same time, he wanted to make sure that Sally would be all right. In case they tried any rough stuff with her, he would be right there, ready to jump in. Sally had the two hundred Golden had given her. There shouldn't be any problem. He waited and watched. When the riders pulled up to the front of the house, Sally waited inside instead of stepping out onto the porch. She and Slocum had planned this all out. She waited for them to step onto the porch and knock on the door. Then she opened it.

"Yes?" she said.

"Tarance and Holland," said one of the men. "We're here to collect the rent for Mr. Smoot."

"Come on in," she said.

She stepped back out of the way and Tarance and Holland came inside.

"Two hundred," said the talker. Sally had no way of knowing who was who and the talker hadn't specified either.

Sally stepped over to a small secretary standing against the wall. She opened the door and pulled out the cash.

"Will you write me a receipt for this?" she asked.

"Sure," said the talker. "Holland, write her a receipt."

Holland pulled a pad out of his pocket and walked over to the table. He put down the pad, took out a pencil and wrote. Then he tore out the page and handed it to Sally. She handed him the cash.

"Let's go," said Tarance.

They walked out the door and closed it behind them. Slocum waited a moment before stepping out into the room with Sally.

"Rude sons of bitches," she said.

"Yeah," said Slocum. He shushed her, and stepped across the room to the front window that was slightly open. Staying to one side, he looked out. Tarance and Holland had reached their horses.

"That was easier than we thought," Tarance said. "Hell, let's split up. That way we'll get done in half the time."

"Good idea," Holland said.

Slocum watched as the two men rode to the gate. Out on the road, Tarance turned to the right, Holland to the left. Slocum had seen Holland pocket the cash, and he was glad to see Holland turn left. He knew that he could ride across Sally's pasture and come out on the road ahead of Holland.

"I'll be back," he said.

"Where are you going?"

"Never mind," he said. "I'll explain when I get back."

He hurried outside and over to the corral, where he saddled his big Appaloosa. Then he mounted up and rode like hell for a place he knew beside the road. He knew he could reach it before Holland did. The Appaloosa flung chunks of pasture behind them like a breeze. Reaching the fence line, Slocum hid the Appaloosa behind some thick brush there. He looked around until he spotted a fist-sized rock lying on the ground. He picked it up and hefted it for feel. Then he moved right up to the fence to wait. In a couple of minutes, Holland came riding along casually. Slocum crouched low behind the bramble. Holland drew alongside him. He waited. Holland rode past.

Slocum stepped out of the brush, drew back his arm and flung the rock through the air. It made a horrible-sounding smack as it struck Holland just above and behind his left ear. He toppled out of his saddle like a dead man. Slocum ducked to step through the wire fence. He hurried out into the road and checked Holland. He was alive but out cold. Quickly Slocum went through Holland's pocket until he found the two hundred dollars. He took it, went back across the fence, mounted up and headed back for the Clay ranch house.

Sally was waiting as Slocum stepped back into the front room of her small house.

"Well?" she said. "What have you been up to?"

He pulled the cash out of his pocket and handed it back to her. Her eyes opened wide.

"Did you kill him?" she said.

"Nope, and he never saw a thing."

"Well, I'll be damned. All right. Let's ride over to Bradley's and give Sammy his money back. I don't like being beholden to anyone longer than I have to."

"Okay," he said. "Let's go."

At the Ringy Dingy, they found Sam Golden sitting on the porch with Julie Bradley. As they dismounted, Golden and Julie stood up to greet them, then offered them chairs to sit in. As they all sat down, Sally pulled the cash out of a pocket and handed it to Golden.

"What's this?" he said. "You need this to pay the rent."

"It's paid," she said. "I've got a receipt."

"You don't need this anymore? You sure?"

"I'm sure. I'm set for a month. Thanks, Sam."

"Well, all right," he said, pocketing the money, "but I don't understand."

"I don't either," Sally said. "All I know is—"

"Never mind about that," said Slocum. "The less any of you know, the better."

"Well then," said Julie, "how are things going over at your place?"

"Slocum's been a great help," Sally said. "The fence is all mended. My cattle are all back where they belong."

"I mean to start on the roof today," Slocum said.

"I ain't so sure about that," said Sally. "Why should you go to so much trouble fixing the place up when I might could wind up losing it all to that damn Smoot?"

"Even if he wins this fight," Slocum said, "the things inside the house belong to you. I don't want your stuff getting ruined by a surprise thunderstorm. I mean to fix the roof."

"All right," Sally said, "but if that son of a bitch gets my place after all this, I'll torch the house and run off the cattle."

"We're going to do everything we can to keep that from happening," said Slocum.

"Damn right," said Golden. "We'll hang onto these places or die trying."

It was early evening before Tarance returned to the headquarters of Smoot there on Sam Golden's ranch. Tarance got back ahead of Holland, and he turned in all the cash he had collected, along with a list of the ranchers he had collected from.

"Where's the rest?" Smoot asked. "And where's Holland?"

"He ought to be along anytime now," Tarance said. "We went up to the widda's place and got her rent. When we seen how easy it was going to be, we decided to split the list up between the two of us. That way, we figured we'd get the job done in half the time. We was right. I didn't have no trouble with none of them."

Just then Holland walked through the door on wobbly legs, holding the side of his head.

"What's wrong with you?" asked Smoot, coming to his feet.

"I don't know," said Holland. "Something hit me. When I come to way later, I was laying in the road. Then I had to find my horse and catch him up, and it weren't easy the way I was feeling. When I finally got mounted up again, I just come straight back here. I ain't feeling so good yet."

"When did this happen?" Smoot asked.

"Right after we left the Clay place," Holland said. "I feel like I'm going to pass out again."

Tarance stepped up close to Holland to examine the side of his head there where he was holding it.

"Ow," Holland said. "That hurts."

"He's got a hell of a knot there," Tarance said. "And his hair's all clotted up with blood."

"You mean you didn't get around to no ranches after you left the Widda Clay's place?" Smoot said.

"Hell no," said Holland. "We left her place and something hit me. That's all I know."

"Well, shit," said Smoot. "All right. Where's the money you collected from her?"

Holland felt his pockets.

"It's gone," he said. "I been robbed."

"Damn it," said Smoot. "You collected from her, and then someone robbed you. Who was there at her place with her?"

"She was there alone," Tarance said.

"Shit," said Smoot. "She couldn't a done this. How'd it happen?"

"I don't know," said Holland. "I was just riding along minding my own business. The next thing I know I'm waking up laying in the road, and my head hurts like hell. That's all I know."

"It's like someone hit him upside the head," said Tarance.

"How could that happen and him riding along like that?"

Tarance shrugged.

"Well, damn it," said Smoot, "tomorrow you go out again and finish the job, but this time don't go splitting up again like that. Be sure the two of you sticks together. You hear me?"

"It went all right with me," Tarance said.

"Just do what I tell you."

"All right."

"I don't know if I can go tomorrow," Holland said. "I feel sick."

"Hell, go on to bed then. I'll send someone else along with Tarance. Go on. Damn it."

Holland wobbled out of the room, as Smoot paced the floor angrily. Suddenly he turned on Tarance.

"Did you give the widda a receipt?"

"She asked for it," Tarance said. "Like you said, we give it."

"Damn. Well, go pick out one of the boys to ride with you tomorrow, and remember what I said. Don't split up. Tell Art and Ned I want to see them right now."

"Okay, Boss," said Tarance, and he turned and walked out of the room.

Smoot paced the floor until Art and Ned came in. Then he sat behind the big desk and lit a cigar. He puffed vigorously for a moment. Then he spoke.

"You hear what happened out there today?" he asked.

"Yeah," said Art. "Ole Holland was crying around out there in the bunkhouse."

"Well, God damn it, I'm sure that damn widda had something to do with it, but there ain't no way I can prove it. I hate getting robbed like that. So we'll take it back in cows. Are you two ready to go?"

"Soon as it's full dark," Ned said.

"Now listen," said Smoot, "see if you can get them cows out without cutting no fence. You hear? If you have to cut fence, don't cut it where it's on the line between that property and this here. Cut it somewhere else. And cover your tracks. I don't want no one to follow no tracks to over here. You got that? We done had one fuckup. I don't want another one."

Smoot poured himself a glass of whiskey. Art and Ned were well on their way to the Widda Clay's place to steal some cattle. He tried to assess his situation. His men had failed to collect all the rent due that day, but hell, the job could be finished up tomorrow. He tried to calm himself down. After all, everything was going his way. In a short time, he would be a very wealthy man. He leaned back in his chair to relax, and Tarance came hurrying into the room. Smoot sat up straight again.

"What is it?" he asked.

"Billy Bob just come back from town," Tarance said. "He was in the saloon, and he overheard some talk. Some of the ranchers. Seems they got together and agreed to pay the first month's rent just to buy them some time. Seems Lawyer Grimes has gone to the capital to get something they called a stay against you. If he gets it filed, you'll have to back off everything and wait till the whole business gets back in court somewheres."

"Damn it," Smoot said, jumping up out of his chair. "We'll

never win in no real court. We might have to take what we
got and clear out of here."

"Hold on, Boss," Tarance said. "Grimes won't get into the
capital till tomorrow night. A man on a good horse could beat
him there. Might kill the horse, but he could beat him there."

"Take two horses," Smoot said. "Get there before that stage.
Stop Grimes. Whatever it takes, stop him. I'll get someone
else to collect the rent tomorrow. You go stop Grimes. I'll pay
you good for this. Here."

He pulled some bills out of the desk drawer and handed
them to Tarance.

"This should cover you till you get back. Go on now. Don't
waste no time."

"I'll stop him, Boss," Tarance. "Don't worry."

Under cover of darkness, Art and Ned rode quietly through
the front gate onto the Clay ranch. As soon as they got in,
they turned sharply to ride the fence line, thereby keeping as
far away from the house as they could to avoid being detected
by the Widow Clay or anyone else who might be there. It took
them a while, but they managed to reach the back pasture
unseen. They found a small herd of cattle grazing there. They
were near the fence line, but just across the fence was the
Golden spread, the land that Smoot was using as his headquarters.

"We can make this real easy," Art said. "Cut that fence and
run them right through there real slick like. No one will see
or hear nothing."

"But the boss said—"

"Hold on, Ned. We run them through there, then from the
other side, we mend the fence back. Then we wipe out the
tracks, and we run the cows way on over to the far side of
the ranch. No one'll be the wiser. Not even the boss."

"Ah, I don't know."

"How else we going to get them over there? We drive a
herd a cattle back to that front gate, someone at the house is
going to hear us."

"I ain't got no tools for fence-mending," Ned said.

"I got everything we need in my saddlebags," said Art. "What do you say?"

Ned thought about it for a moment. It would be a lot simpler and much quicker. He wanted to get back to the bunkhouse.

"Let's do it," he said.

The fence was quickly cut, and the two rustlers began the work of driving the cattle through. They rode among the previously contented creatures swinging their ropes, causing them to run and bawl. Back and forth they rode, driving through a few head at a time. Finally, Ned said, "That's enough, ain't it?"

Art agreed. They rode on through the fence, dismounted, and began their work on the sabotaged wire. Art let a wire slip, and a sharp barb cut through his glove and into his palm.

"Shit," he said.

Working together as fast as they could in the dark, the two scoundrels finally got the wire restretched and retacked.

"What about the tracks?" asked Ned.

"You get a brush clump and go back across," Art said. "Sweep them tracks out over there. While you're doing that, I'll ride back and forth along the fence here and tramp out all the cow tracks."

"Okay."

That little chore took quite some time. Ned was getting frustrated.

"Damn it," he said. "We shoulda drove them beeves out some other way like the boss told us to do. This is too damn much work."

"That's enough," said Art. "Hell, them tracks is all wiped out by now. Come on. Let's drive them cows away from this side."

Slocum had spent the remainder of the day patching the roof on the small ranch house. It was late. He had started to head for the barn, but Sally had called him into the house. He thought that she was going to offer him a cup of coffee, but when he sat down at the table, she produced a bottle of whiskey from a cabinet and set it on the table. Then she brought out two glasses. She sat down across from him.

"Like a drink, cowboy?" she said.

"I never turn down a drink of good whiskey offered by a beautiful lady," he said.

Sally poured the two glasses full. She lifted hers as if for a toast, and Slocum did the same.

"To the downfall of Smoot," she said.

"To your success," Slocum said.

They each took a drink, and Slocum noted that her whiskey was good. He also decided that he liked her even more than before.

"Slocum," she said, "if it wasn't for you, I don't know where I'd be right this minute. I was ready to give it all up whenever ole Bradley come over and brought you and Sam along with him. I don't know how to thank you."

"Don't worry about it," Slocum said. "It was Sammy that brought me into this. I'm glad he did though. I'm glad to be of some help."

"You've been a lot of help," she said, "and besides that, it's just been good having you around the place. Slocum, there's no need for you to go to the barn to sleep tonight."

"Sally," he said, "when this trouble is all over with, I'll be riding on."

"I know that," she said.

6

She took him by the hand and led him into her bedroom. A lantern sat on a table against the wall. She struck a match and lit it, then adjusted the flame, not too light, not too dark. Then, standing beside the bed, she looked at him and slowly began undressing. He stood across the bed from her, and he picked up her cue by pulling off his shirt. Soon they stared at one another across the clean sheets, both as naked as the day they were born. Slocum took her in. She was no spring chicken. He knew that. But she had a shapely body still. Better than more than a few young women he had known. Sally's was a body kept slim and trim where it should be and round in all the right places from hard work. She was a ranch woman, and it showed.

She was studying him too. He could tell. He hoped that she was liking what she saw as much as he was liking the sight of her. Almost as if on a signal, each put a knee on the bed. They moved toward one another. On their knees, they came together in the middle of the mattress. They pressed their bodies together and wrapped their arms around one another. Their lips met in a lingering kiss. Slocum's hands moved around feeling Sally's smooth back, and he thrilled at her touch. He slid his hands down to clutch a round ass cheek in each one. Then he felt his cock rising to the occasion. All on its own, it nudged Sally between the legs, feeling the damp tangled hair, the warm softness of the waiting and anxious silky lips.

"Oh, Slocum," she said.

She moved her hands to his chest, then slid them down his stomach and even lower until she reached the throbbing rod. One hand went beneath it to cup the heavy balls. The other gripped the shaft and squeezed it. Slowly she stroked the wild cock, and it began to buck in her hand. Slocum took her in his arms and lowered her onto her back. Her legs opened wide to accept him there, and as he moved into position, she guided the tool into her hungry hole. It slipped in easily, and he drove it all the way.

Sally gasped and arched her back.

"Fuck me, Slocum," she said. "Fuck me hard."

And he did. He pounded himself against her again and again, driving his rod deep into her cavernous love tunnel, pumping harder and faster with each stroke until he had to slow it down. He was panting, and so was she. He lay heavy on top of her, breathing into her ear, the sweat of their bodies mingling together.

"Slocum," she said finally, "get behind me. Mount me like an old bull on a cow."

She was a ranch woman all right. He backed off and out, raising his body to allow her free movement, and she rolled over and got up on hands and knees, displaying to him her lovely round ass. He moved up close against it, and she reached back between her legs and grasped his tool again, guiding it into her slippery hole. Slocum drove it home. She wriggled her butt with delight, and Slocum had to hold hard to her hips to keep from losing his saddle as he pounded into her again and again. At last the pressure was too great. He could no longer hold it back, and he spurted into her again and again. They both stopped still and held the position. Slowly, Slocum's tool withered until it at last slipped free. He lay down beside her on his back with a loud and satisfied sigh. She snuggled down against him, her head on his chest, her hand stroking his slimy, spent cock.

"I needed that," she said. "But the next time, if you'll let me, I'll ride you."

"Lady," said Slocum, "you can ride me anytime you want to."

*   *   *

Tarance had ridden hard, and he managed to catch up to the stagecoach about half a day before it would have arrived at the capital. Luck was with him, he thought. He had been worrying about just how he would deal with the problem if Grimes made it to the city ahead of him. He passed the stage off the road to avoid being seen. Then he switched horses, leaving the one he had just ridden hard to graze and rest up some. He tied a bandana over his face, pulled out a six-gun and rode down to the edge of the road.

When the stage rounded the bend, he came out quick beside it, his revolver leveled at the guard up on the box.

"Hold up there," he shouted.

The shotgun was too surprised to react quickly. He held up his hands. The driver stopped the horses and set the brake.

"We ain't carrying nothing of any value, mister," the driver said.

"I'll be the judge of that," Tarance said. "Throw down your weapons."

The shotgun rider tossed out a shotgun, a six-gun and a rifle.

"That's all," he said.

Tarance turned his head toward the passenger door.

"Everyone out," he said.

Two women, one young and one older, squealed as they disembarked. A man with the look of a rancher stepped out, holding his hands high. Then Lawyer Grimes emerged. Tarance poked the barrel of his shooter at Grimes.

"Step over there," he said, gesturing to the side of the road.

Grimes moved away from the other passengers.

"The rest of you get back in," said Tarance. They did. "Drive on."

The driver whipped up the horses, and the stage rumbled on down the road, leaving the shotgun guard's weapons there in the dirt. Tarance watched it for a spell, then turned back on Grimes. "Get going," he said, gesturing the direction. Grimes started walking, and Tarance rode along slowly behind him. In a few minutes, they came to Tarance's extra horse. "Get on that horse," Tarance said.

"What's this all about?" Grimes asked. "I don't have much cash on me, but—"

"Shut up," said Tarance, "and mount up."

They rode on a few miles, heading into the wide-open spaces well away from the road. Then Tarance called a halt. He told Grimes to dismount. Then he climbed off his horse. He gathered the reins of both horses and cocked his revolver.

"What the hell is this?" Grimes demanded.

"What you know or don't know don't matter now," Tarance said, pulling down the bandana down to reveal his face. He grinned, an evil, gap-toothed grin. "Mr. Smoot don't want you filing no papers at the capital."

The blast and the stench from Tarance's forty-four filled the air on the open prairie, and Grimes fell back dead, a gaping hole in his chest. The spooked horses started to dance, and Tarance fought to control them. When he at last had them settled again, he quickly went through the dead man's pockets, taking out every paper he found. He also took what cash he found. He stuffed it all into his own pockets. Then he mounted up and headed back for the Smoot headquarters. He felt good. He had done his job.

Golden rode out with Julie for a pleasant afternoon. The weather was nice, and they were enjoying one another's company. They passed through small herds of grazing cattle. Now and then they came on cowhands at work, and they slowed down to greet them and visit with them a bit. They remarked to one another about the beauty of the countryside, the richness of the range land. Carefully, they avoided any unpleasant talk about the ugly business with Smoot, and the possibility that they would lose their homes or have to fight and stain the land with blood.

But before they realized what they had done, they found themselves looking across a fence at Golden's place. They stopped and sat in their saddles quietly for a long moment, staring at the land that should be his. Cattle grazed contentedly over there. Golden heaved a sigh.

"Are those my cows?" he asked.

"I guess they should be," Julie said.

"Ah, let's get away from here," he said.

"Wait a minute," said Julie.

"Why?" he said. "What's wrong?"

"Smoot's no cow man," she said. "He's just been using your place for an outlaw headquarters is all. Come on."

She kicked her mount in the sides and headed for the fence. Golden followed her. They stopped right at the fence, and Julie squinted her eyes, studying the cattle on Golden's side.

"I wish they were a little closer," she said.

"Julie," he said, "I wish you'd tell me what you're up to."

She dismounted and handed her reins to Golden.

"Hold my horse, Sammy," she said. Before he could protest any further, she had ducked through the wire fence and was walking toward the cattle.

"Julie," he called out. "Be careful."

"There's no one over here," she said without breaking her stride. Closer to the cattle, she stopped. A moment later, she turned and headed back for the fence. Ducking through again, she walked over to her horse and climbed back into the saddle. "I was right," she said.

"About what?"

"Those are not Smoot's cows, and they're not yours."

"Well, then, whose are they?"

"They're wearing Sally Clay's brand," she said. "Come on. Let's ride over and see her."

Slocum was out back chopping stove wood when Golden and Julie rode up. Sally invited them in, called out for Slocum, and poured coffee all around.

"I've got some good apple pie," she said. "Have a slab?"

By the time Slocum came in and said howdy and got seated, Sally had sliced pie for everyone. Then she sat down.

"This is good," Golden said. "Say, you need another hand over here?"

Julie gave him a hard look.

"Something wrong with my pies?" she said.

"Now, I didn't mean that," Golden said.

Sally chuckled.

"It really is good," Julie said, smiling. "I just thought that Sammy needed some ribbing."

"Likely he needs more than that," said Slocum.

Julie took a sip of coffee and put her cup down.

"Sally," she asked, "have you sold any cattle lately?"

"Now where would I be selling cows around here this time of year?" Sally replied.

"Then you haven't?"

"No. How come you to ask me that?"

"There's some cows wearing your brand over on Smoot's place, I mean, Sammy's place. We just saw them."

Sally looked from Julie to Slocum, then back at Julie.

"You sure?"

"Hell," said Golden, "she crawled through the fence to get a closer look."

"Even if I had sold any, which I ain't, I wouldn't have sold them to that son of a bitch," Sally said.

"Is there any way he could've bought them from someone else?" Slocum asked.

"No way," Sally said. She stood up and pulled off her apron, wiped her mouth and hands on it, and threw it down on the table.

"Where you going?" Slocum asked.

"I ain't going off half-cocked," she said. "I'm going out and riding my range. I'll see if my critters are all here. When I've done that, I'm riding over to the Ringy Dingy." She looked at Julie. "With your permission, a course."

"You have it," Julie said.

"Then I'll ride out to where they seen my cows, and I'll have my own look. I'll be able to say from personal knowledge that them's my cattle over there."

"What then?" Slocum asked.

"Since we're all being so God damned careful around here," she said, "I'll go report it to the sheriff. We'll see what he does about it. If anything. That meet with everyone's approval?"

"Sounds good to me," Slocum said. "I'll ride along."

Julie gave Golden a quick look.

"We will too," she said.

"Yeah," Golden said.

The day was done by the time they had ridden Sally's range and then gone to see the cattle there where Julie had seen them. They had not strayed far, and Sally had been able to get a good look herself.

"The son of a bitch has rustled my herd," she said. "That's for sure."

"What's he up to, Slocum?" Golden said. "He seems to think that he owns the whole valley anyhow. Why would he go to stealing cattle?"

"That's a good question, Sam," Slocum said. "Maybe he thinks that Grimes is going to win this thing for you ranchers, and he's looking for ways to make him some more money before he has to clear out. Or maybe he wants this valley cleared out of ranchers, and he's picking on the smallest and weakest ones first. He don't know anything about me being over at Sally's place. Likely, he thinks he got her last two hundred dollars, and now he's got half her cows. The way it looks from where he stands, Sally's likely to give it all up and ride out of here. Whover he thinks is next in line, that is, the next most vulnerable, he'll probably strike there next."

"Damn," Golden said. "He's lower than a snake in the grass."

"I ain't leaving, Slocum," Sally said. "I can take a loss as good as anyone, if it's an honest fight, but if Smoot wins this and takes over my place, he'll have to bury me on it."

"I don't think that would bother him a bit," Slocum said, "but we got to try to keep it from happening, to you or any other rancher in this valley."

Tarance walked into the big living room of the larcenous Smoot headquarters. He found Smoot behind the big desk. Smoot looked up anxiously. Tarance pulled papers out of his pockets as he walked over to the desk. Reaching it, he began tossing them down on the desktop. Greedily, Smoot grabbed up the papers to examine them.

"Does this mean—"

"He ain't never filing no papers again," Tarance said. "Except maybe in hell."

"Great," said Smoot. "That was our biggest problem. You're sure now that he didn't get anything filed before you got to him?"

"He never made it to the capital," said Tarance.

"That's fine. That's just fine." Smoot reached into a drawer for some bills, which he handed to Tarance. "Here. You earned it. Sit down. We'll have us a drink to celebrate."

Tarance sat as Smoot got the bottle and glasses. Smoot poured and handed a glass to Tarance. Then he offered Tarance a cigar, and both men lit up, and kicked back to relax.

"What's next, Boss?" Tarance asked.

"Most of the rent's been collected," Smoot said. "Some of the other boys can handle that all right. Last night, I had Art and Ned run off some of the Widda Clay's cows. I think what's best is for you to join up with them two tomorrow night—get yourself a good rest tonight—go with them to hit ole Chester Welch's place. Next to the widda, he's probably the hurtinest one in the valley. We break the backs of these smallest ones and get them outa here, then we can really concentrate our efforts on the big ones like Bradley."

"Who's going to be in charge of this cow gathering trio?"

"Why, you are, of course," said Smoot.

Tarance grinned.

"I'll get the job done," he said.

It was too late in the evening to go to town to see the sheriff, so Julie invited Slocum and Sally to spend the night at the Ringy Dingy.

"I appreciate that," Sally said, "but I think we'd best get on back to my place. The bastards didn't run off all my cows. They might come back for the rest. I want to be watching."

"You going into Harleyville in the morning then?" Golden asked.

"First thing," Sally said.

"Slow down on your way past here," said Golden. "We'll ride in with you."

"See you then."

Sally and Slocum mounted up and headed back toward Sally's ranch. For a while they rode in silence. The night sky was well lit by a bright nearly full moon and millions of twinkling stars. It was clear of clouds. The weather was still pleasant. They rode along at a leisurely pace.

"I do want to make sure no one comes after the rest of my cows," Sally said at last.

"It's a good idea," said Slocum.

"But that ain't the only reason I turned down the offer to stay the night."

"Oh?"

"No, it ain't. I was kinda afraid that Julie might stick us in different rooms for the night."

"I don't know what difference that would've made," said Slocum, "if we're going to be up all night long nursemaiding cows."

"It might not make no difference tonight," Sally said, "but it was the idea of the thing. We get on back home, the choice is ours, not someone else's."

7

It was about mid-morning the next day when Slocum, Sally, Golden and Julie rode up in front of the sheriff's office in Harleyville. They dismounted and tied their horses to the hitch rail there, then went inside. Sheriff Potter looked up from behind his desk as they stepped in.

"Morning, folks," he said. "What can I do for you?"

Sally stalked to the center of the desk.

"Some of Smoot's men ran off about half my herd night before last," she said.

"Hold on there," said Potter. "Did you see them do it?"

"I seen the cows on his range," Sally said.

"On what he's calling his range," Golden said.

"That's right," said Julie. "I saw them first. I was on my side of the fence, and the cattle were on the other side. They were close to the fence, so I could see the brand. Sammy here was with me."

"That's right," Golden said. "So we rode over to tell Sally."

"Then me and Slocum joined up with these two. We rode my range first, and I seen that about half my herd was missing. Then we rode with them back over to the Ringy Dingy, and all four of us seen my cows. Smoot's got them over on that range all right, the range he's using as his headquarters."

Potter shoved his chair back and stood up. He walked over to where his gun belt hung from a peg on the wall.

"With four witnesses," he said, "I reckon I got cause enough to ride out there and take a look for myself."

"We'll ride with you," said Sally.

"I'd rather you didn't do that," Potter said. "I ain't looking to get a big fight started here. With just me going out to look, there's a better chance that it'll stay peaceful. You all go on back to your own ranches. I'll let you know what's going on."

"You go out there and you'll see my cows," said Sally. "Once you see them, you'll have reason to put that son of a bitch in jail."

"I'll keep you informed of what's happening," Potter said.

"Let's go, Sally," said Slocum.

"Oh, all right."

The four visitors went back outside and mounted up. Potter came out just behind them. He closed the office door and locked it. Then he started walking toward the stable at the far end of the street.

"Well, what do you think?" Golden asked.

"He ain't done us no good so far," said Sally.

"But there hasn't been anything he could do," Julie said. "He had to do what the judge ordered. Stolen cattle is a different matter entirely. I believe Sheriff Potter is an honest man and means to do what's right."

"I'm afraid my faith in law and order has been pretty well shattered," Sally said, "but I reckon we'll wait and see."

"It'll be about noon by the time we get back," said Julie. "Why don't you two stop and eat with us?"

Slocum looked at Sally.

"Sounds good to me," she said. "Thanks."

Riding along the road at a leisurely pace, Slocum and Sally dropped back behind the other two, allowing them to get a good distance ahead.

"Look at them two," Sally said. "They sure seem to be getting cozy with each other. You reckon something'll come of that?"

"If it don't," Slocum said, "it won't be 'cause ole Sammy didn't try. I do believe he's really took with that gal. I could see it from almost the first time we met her."

"Well, they couldn't neither one of them do no better, the way I see it," Sally said. "They're good kids."

"The only problem I see is that they're trying to get together here in the big middle of a passel of trouble," Slocum said. "I hope they both come through it all right."

"Yeah," Sally said. "Me too."

"Now, I hope you come through it all right too," he said, "and I mean to do all I can to see that everything turns out right for all of you."

Sally leaned sideways and reached over to pat Slocum's hand where it rested on the saddle horn. At the same time, she smiled up into his face.

"I know you do, cowboy," she said. "I know you do."

The four pards were already seated at the table in the head-quarters of the Ringy Dingy by the time Sheriff Potter rode up to the house where Smoot was staying. Tarance was standing on the porch. He grinned.

"Howdy, Sheriff," he said. "Something we can do for you here?"

"I need to see Smoot," said Potter, climbing down off his horse.

"What about?"

"That's between me and him." Potter hitched his horse to the rail and started up the stairs. "Is he in there?"

Tarance moved to stand in Potter's way.

"Well, now, he might be, and then he might not be. Maybe you'd oughta tell me what this is all about."

"I told you, it's between me and Smoot. Are you going to get out of my way?"

Tarance smirked out loud, then turned and stepped to the door. He opened it a crack and stuck in his nose.

"Hey, Boss," he called out. "You taking visitors?"

Potter could hear Smoot's answer from inside the house. "Who is it?"

"The sheriff from Harleyville."

In another few seconds, the door was pulled open from inside, and Smoot was standing in the doorway, a broad smile across his face.

"Come in," he said, sticking out his hand for Potter to shake. Potter stepped inside, past Tarance, ignoring the hand.

"This ain't a social call," he said.

"Sit down," said Smoot, indicating a chair.

Potter sat, and Smoot walked over to his desk, picking up a cigar box and opening it.

"Have one," he said, holding the box toward Potter. Potter declined.

"I have four witnesses who say they saw some of Sally Clay's cattle on your range here," he said. "What do you know about that?"

"Why, nothing," Smoot said, a feigned look of surprise on his face. "Who said that?"

"Never mind who," Potter said. "I came out here to ride out and look over the cattle on the place. Any objections?"

"Of course not," said Smoot. "I have nothing to hide. If you should find any of the widda's cows, let me know. I'll have some of the boys drive them back over to her place for her. I can't imagine how they got here. In fact, I think there's been some mistake. But go look, by all means. Look as much as you want."

Potter stood up.

"I'll do that," he said. "Right now."

"Stop back by the house when you're done," Smoot said.

"You can be sure of that."

Potter went out the door, and Smoot stood watching, a hard scowl on his ugly face. In a moment he stepped to the door to look out. Potter was just disappearing around the corner of the house. Tarance still stood on the porch like a snarling guard dog. Smoot stepped on out to stand beside his cur.

"Follow him," he said. "If he should run onto any of the widda's cows, leave him out there with them."

Tarance, without a word, stepped off the porch and headed for the corral.

It was a big ranch, rivaling the Ringy Dingy, and Potter rode for some time without seeing any cattle. He did finally see a small cluster of cows, not enough to call a herd, and he rode in close. He checked each animal carefully, but he found that they all wore the brand of the late owner of the place. They belonged to either Smoot or Golden, depending on how this damned case finally worked out in the courts. Potter knew that Grimes had gone to the capital in order to obtain a stay against Smoot until he could get the case back in court. He wished that the lawyer would hurry up and get the thing resolved, hopefully in favor of the original owners. He rode on toward another section of the range.

He reached a wooded area with a stream and a pond. It was a likely place for cattle to gather. Riding around the woods, he saw a small herd there grazing contentedly. He rode toward them slowly, not wanting to spook them. The scene was peaceful, belying the tension that was building up in the valley. He moved carefully in among the cattle, and he saw the brand. It was Sally Clay's all right. No doubt about it. Knowing what Smoot would say, had already said, in fact, he decided to check the fence line to see if there was any chance the cattle had strayed onto the place. But just then he heard something behind him. He turned to see Tarance riding up.

"Howdy again," said Tarance, riding up close.

"Did Smoot send you?"

"He sure enough did."

"Well," Potter said, "you can see for yourself. These are Sally Clay's cattle. I'm going to ride the fence line to see if there's any place they could have strayed over here. Ride along with me if you like."

"I'll just do that."

"Your boss said that he'd send some of the boys to drive these cows home if I found them here," Potter said. He was turning his mount to head toward the property's edge.

"That'll be the day," Tarance said, as he slipped the revolver from his holster. Potter turned his head to look over his shoulder.

"What?" he said. He saw the gun aimed at his back, saw Tarance thumb back the hammer. He knew at that instant that everything the ranchers had been saying about Smoot was true, knew that the man was a crook, a rustler and a swindler. He knew it all, but it was too late. Tarance pulled the trigger.

*　　*　　*

It was two days later when Sally's patience ran out.

"Slocum," she said, "saddle up. We're going to town."

"What for?"

"We're going to see that damn Potter," she said. "He's had plenty of time to ride that whole range over there, and if he rode it, he saw my cows. Why ain't he come out to see me? Well, I ain't waiting any longer for him."

Out in the corral as Slocum was tightening the cinch on his saddle, he asked Sally, "You want to stop by for Sam and Julie?"

"No need to bother them," she said.

"Well, they were with us at the beginning of this," he said. "I'm thinking that they're interested too."

"Oh, all right."

He decided to be real careful what he said or how he said it. Sally was on a real tear. If he didn't hold his mouth just right, he could set her off. They mounted up and headed to town. They did stop by the Ringy Dingy, and Golden and Julie saddled up and joined them. The four of them rode toward town together.

In Harleyville, they found the sheriff's office locked.

"Well," Slocum said. "What now?"

"Start asking around," Sally said.

It didn't take long. They found out that no one in Harleyville had seen Potter for the last two days, since, in fact, Slocum figured, he had left to ride out and check on Sally's stolen cattle.

"I don't like this," he told the others.

"What do you think?" Golden asked.

"I don't like to make guesses," Slocum said, "but he went out to see Smoot and look for them cows, and no one's seen him since. Sure sounds suspicious to me."

"Well, what're we going to do?" asked Golden.

"I got me an idea," Slocum said, "but I don't want to talk about it here."

*   *   *

Slocum and Sammy waited for darkness to fall before they set out. Slocum drove the wagon, loaded up with all the fence-mending equipment they would need. They headed out from the Ringy Dingy headquarters, with the complete blessing of old man Bradley. Golden rode horseback, and Slocum's big Appaloosa was tied to the back of the wagon. They rode to the fence line where they had seen Sally's cattle. When they reached the spot, they squinted into the darkness.

"They've moved on," Slocum said.

"There are woods just a couple a miles straight ahead," Golden said. "I can't see it just now, but I seen it in daylight. Looked like a likely place for water to me."

"Maybe they're over there," Slocum said. "Let's check it out."

He set the brake on the wagon and climbed down. He fetched a pair of wire cutters from the wagon and moved over to cut the fence. Then he pulled the wires back out of the way, moved to the back of the wagon, loosened the reins and mounted the Appaloosa.

"Come on, Sammy," he said.

They rode through the fence and headed for the woods. They rode easy. It was dark, and they didn't want to endanger their horses. Besides that, they were in enemy territory. They didn't believe that any of Smoot's gang would be that far out from the ranch house at that time of night, but they didn't want to take any chances. They were slow and careful. They reached the woods and rode around it to the other side, and there they found Sally's small herd. They had to look close for the brands in the darkness.

"It's them all right," Slocum said. "Let's get them moving."

Both men were skilled cattle workers, and each had an experienced horse underneath him. In a short while, they had the herd bunched, and they started moving it toward the hole in the fence. Still they moved slowly. Still they watched all around in case a rider should appear. The cattle bawled as they moved along.

They were moving them through the fence when a young cow kicked up her heels, turned and ran in the wrong direction.

"Slocum," said Golden.

"I see her," Slocum said. "Get the rest of these on through. I'll catch her."

He paid out a loop in his rope as he rode after the ornery cow. She was headed back for the water there by the trees. Hurrying along, he swung his loop. Close enough, he tossed it, and it circled the cow's head, settling around her neck. She ran on, suddenly jerking it tight. Her ass end swung around in front of her at the sudden catch. Slocum turned his horse to head back to the fence with his prize.

Suddenly the Appaloosa balked.

"What is it, big fella?"

The horse would not step forward. Slocum looked at the ground. He could see a form there. Something. Something the horse did not want to step on.

"Hold up," he said. "Keep that rope tight."

He swung down out of the saddle for a closer look, and he found himself staring at the remains of Sheriff Potter.

"Well," he said. "That's that."

He mounted up and took the cow back to the fence and through it to mingle again with the rest of the herd. Turning her loose, he rode back over to where Golden waited.

"Well," Golden said, "shall we get this fence fixed?"

"Sammy," Slocum said, "I found Potter out there."

"Dead?"

"I reckon. Two day's worth. The question now is what should we do about it?"

"It don't seem right to just leave him lying there, do it?" Golden said.

"I think I'll drive the wagon through and load him in it," Slocum said. "We can ask Bradley what to do from there."

"Yeah," said Golden. "Okay."

Slocum drove the wagon back for the body. When he had finished that unpleasant task, he stopped back on the Ringy Dingy side of the fence and helped Golden stretch new wire. When the fence was all mended, with Sally's cattle on the Ringy Dingy side of the fence, they returned to the ranch house. Bradley, Julie and Sally were all still up waiting for them.

"Did you get my cows?" Sally asked.

"Every last one," said Golden. "Mended the fence back too."

"There's something else though," Slocum added.

Everyone could see the solemn look on his face.

"What is it?" Bradley asked.

"I found Potter over there," said Slocum. "He'd been shot in the back. I loaded him into the wagon and brought him along. I don't know if he has any kin around—"

"No," said Bradley, shaking his head, "he don't have. Not that anyone knows of."

"Then I suggest that we bury him quietly somewhere out here on your spread. No sense in taking him to town. There'd be questions asked. If we was to tell the truth, say where we found him, Smoot and his bunch would just say we're lying and try to blame it back on us."

"Slocum," said Bradley, "I think you're right. I'll have Dave get some of the boys to take care of it."

"There's another thing to consider," Slocum said.

"Yes?"

"Right now, till we hear something from that lawyer, Grimes, there ain't no law in these parts. None."

8

Tarance rode out with Art and Ned to round up some more cattle from another of the small ranchers. Smoot had decided to leave Sally alone for a few days. Keep her and the others wondering where the rustlers would hit next. With the law out of the way, he was more relaxed, bolder. Even so, he wanted to keep everyone guessing. So Tarance led the other two rustlers off to the small spread of Simon Stout. It was well after dark by the time they reached the Stout place, and they found that there was no way to reach his cattle without riding past the tumbledown ranch house. They stopped in the road. Tarance was studying the situation.

"Well," Art said finally, "what do we do?"

"We'll ride on in," said Tarance. "Keep as far from the house as we can and move slow. Try to stay quiet."

"That's fine," Ned said, "but what about getting back out with the cattle?"

"We'll deal with that when the time comes," said Tarance. "Come on."

They moved slowly onto the Stout property, riding close to the fence line. When at last they were well beyond the house, they rode along at a faster pace. They would have to ride over Stout's pasture until they came across the cattle. They could be anywhere.

"Good thing it's a small spread," Art said.

Then they came across the small herd.

"Bunch them up and move them out," Tarance said.

They loosened their lariats and rode in among the cattle, winging ropes and whooping. When they had them all together, they began moving them back toward the road. They would have to drive them past the ranch house. It was the only way in or out without getting onto someone else's land, and Tarance did not want to chance that. Not just yet.

"These damn cows is bound to wake ole Stout up," Art said.

"Yeah?" Tarance said. "Well, just keep your eyes on that house whenever we drive them by there."

They moved the bawling herd closer to the road. Then they could see the house. It was all dark.

"Keep your eyes peeled, boys," said Tarance.

The herd sounded much louder to the rustlers' nervous ears as they came even with the sleeping house. They looked from herd to house, but even so, they did not see, in the darkness, the door of the house open up, and the man with a rifle in his hands step into the open doorway. The man raised the rifle to his shoulder. They heard the shot, and they saw Ned fall from his saddle.

"Damn," said Tarance, pulling the rifle from his scabbard. "Get the son of a bitch."

Both outlaws turned rifles on the house. Without a clear view in the darkness, they aim for where they thought the door to be, firing as fast as they could. A bullet whizzed close by Tarance's ear. He cursed again and fired another round at the house. Art pulled his trigger, only to hear a click.

"Shit," he said. "Empty."

Tarance fired two more rounds and ran out. Both men pulled out their six guns, but stopped still. No more shots were coming from the house. All was quiet except for the bawling of the cows.

"You reckon we got him?" asked Art.

"We must have," said Tarance. "Let's get the hell out of here with these cows."

Simon Stout stepped into his doorway from inside the house where he had ducked when the fast shooting began. He watched as the last of his herd was driven away.

"God damn bastards," he muttered.

*   *   *

Sally was dishing out breakfast for herself and Slocum when they heard the rider approaching the house. Slocum got up from the table and stepped over to the door to look out and see Simon Stout riding up. He spoke to Sally over his shoulder.

"It's that Stout feller," he said.

"Invite him in," said Sally. "I'll put out another plate."

Stout came into the house at Slocum's invitation and took a place at the table.

"Thanks, Sally," he said. "I ain't had a good, home-cooked breakfast in a while. I've had home cooked, but it was my cooking, and that ain't good."

"You come over anytime," Sally said.

"I'm obliged to you, and it sure looks and smells worth the ride over, but it ain't why I came."

"Oh?" said Sally. "Why did you come over then?"

"Three men run off my whole herd last night," Stout said. "Ever' last cow."

"Do you know who they were?" Slocum asked.

"I know for sure who one of them was," Stout answered, "on account of I killed the son of a bitch. The other two just rode off and left him lay. It was that Ned that works for Smoot."

"That figures," said Sally. "Smoot's bunch stole half my herd a few nights ago, but I got mine back. I have an idea where we can find them."

She laid out platters of eggs and ham and biscuits, a bowl of gravy, and set cups of steaming coffee all around, and for a while the talk stopped. In a few minutes the platters were all empty, the plates cleaned off and the coffeepot drained.

"What do you think we oughta do about Simon's herd, Slocum?" Sally asked.

"Let's all ride over and have a talk with ole Bradley," he suggested.

In the big ranch house on the Ringy Dingy, Slocum, Sally and Stout sat down with ole Bradley, Dave, Julie and Golden. Julie served coffee all around. Stout told his story, and for a moment everyone was silent. Then old Bradley spoke out.

"I've got plenty of grazing land and plenty of water," he said. "I've got extra room here in the house and out at the bunkhouse. What I'm thinking is that we ought to drive all the herds in the valley onto the Ringy Dingy. Come roundup time, we'll want to get them all together anyhow for the drive. Then all the ranchers can move out here. That way there'll be plenty of us to watch the cattle around the clock. The numbers, all consolidated right here, will give us strength. We can hold out like that till Grimes gets back and we get this thing all settled."

Again there was silence.

"Well," said Stout, "It sounds all right. Course, it's too late for me. My herd's gone."

"So was half a mine," Sally said, "but we got it back. What do you say, Slocum?"

"About the plan?" he said. "It's a good one. With everyone all scattered out through the valley, we never know where they might hit next. This way, like Mr. Bradley says, we can watch all the cattle all the time."

"About Simon's herd?" Sally asked.

"I reckon we can get it back."

All of them, even old Bradley, saddled up and went for a ride. They rode to the spot where Slocum and Golden had cut the fence to drive Sally's cattle through. They did not immediately see any cattle on the other side.

"If they brought them in the way they did the last time," Golden said, "they might be over yonder behind them trees."

"So what do we do about it?" Stout asked.

"The only way we can get over there and check is by cutting this fence and then mending the damn thing again," Slocum said.

"That's how we done it the last time," Golden said.

"That's your ranch over there, Sam," said Bradley. "Right?"

"Yes, sir."

"What do you say we put a gate right here?"

Golden grinned.

"I'd say that's a fine idea," he said.

"Dave," Bradley said, "send some of the boys out here to take care of that little chore. Some of us can get started riding around the valley to tell everyone our plan. We'll keep some of the crew busy getting ready for the crowd. We'll try to start moving them all in early in the morning."

"What about Simon's cattle?" Sally asked.

"The gate'll be in place before dark," Bradley said. "After dark some of us can go over there and find them. Drive them through to this side."

Just as Bradley said, the gate was finished well before dark. Its chain latch was secured by a padlock to keep any of Smoot's men from making easy use of it. The raid for Stout's herd was made much easier as a result of the gate. Slocum, Dave, Golden and Stout found the cattle after a short ride and drove them easily through the gate. They closed and locked the gate behind them. Stout rode on home after that. He would gather up what was necessary and return to the Ringy Dingy in the morning. Slocum and Sally went back to Sally's ranch.

"You think we need to watch the herd tonight?" she asked him.

"If they come and get them," he said, "they'll just have done our work for us. Instead of having to drive them all the way over to Bradley's range, all we'll have to do is go through the gate and fetch them in."

Sally laughed.

"That's right," she said. "Then let's you and me just relax for the rest of the night. We'll have plenty of work to do in the morning."

The rustlers did not strike that night, and the following morning, small herds of cattle were being driven along all the roads and trails in the valley, all headed for the Ringy Dingy. Ahead of them or in their wake, wagons rolled, loaded down with supplies. The entire valley seemed to be in the midst of a chaotic mass migration. From their headquarters on Sam Golden's ranch, Smoot and Tarance could hear some of the commotion.

"Ride out there and see what the hell's going on," Smoot said.

In a few minutes, Tarance was on the road. He had to move off to one side soon, however, when a herd of bawling cattle came at him. He got out of their way, waited and watched until they had passed him by, then followed, eating their dust and cursing to himself. He followed until he saw the herd being driven onto the Ringy Dingy. While he watched another came from the opposite direction. Yet a third came following in the tracks of the first herd he had watched. He turned his horse and rode out to look over some more of the valley. Several hours later, Tarance pulled up in front of Smoot's headquarters. He dismounted and went inside.

"Well," Smoot asked, "what's going on?"

"It looks like the whole damn valley has packed up and moved onto Bradley's place," Tarance said.

"What?"

"I mean ever' cow and ever' last human bein'. All the little ranches is deserted. All the rangeland is bare. All 'cept for the Ringy Dingy. They're all gathered up there."

"It sounds like they're getting ready for war," Smoot said. "Well, by God, we'll give it to them."

"We ain't got enough men to fight the whole valley at once and all in one place," Tarance said. "It was okay the way it was, but with them all bunched up like that, well, I don't know."

"Then we'll get more men," said Smoot. "How many more you reckon we need?"

"At least a dozen good guns," Tarance said.

"That many?"

"We'd still be outnumbered, but some of them ranchers ain't shucks with firearms. Give me a dozen more good men, and I can fight the whole damn valley."

"You know where to find them?"

"I can round up a dozen," said Tarance.

"All right," Smoot said. "Get to it."

The Ringy Dingy looked like a new town site following a land run. There were wagons and horses and people everywhere. The cattle had all been driven to the far range, and four cowhands, including Dave Bradley, were riding herd and watching for rustlers. Back at the ranch house, Bradley, Slocum, Golden, Sally and Julie sat on the porch. Everyone there except Julie had a glass of whiskey. Golden noticed that, and even though he had accepted a glass, he sipped it slowly, not wanting to have a refill. He did not want to do anything that might offend Julie, and if she was not having a drink, he would not drink very much. Just one to be sociable. That would be enough.

"We're going to win this thing," Bradley said. "Hell, it would take an army to get in here and get at us."

"You've still got to win it in the courts," Slocum said. "You can't run this place indefinitely with everyone here like this."

"Grimes'll be back in a week," Bradley said. "We'll win all right. And Smoot'll find his ass in prison or else hanging from a branch by the neck."

"Wonder how the bastard is taking all this?" Sally said.

"You suppose he's figured out what we're up to?" asked Julie.

"He's likely figured it out by now," said Slocum, "and I'd bet he's taking it pretty hard."

Then he mused and muttered, apparently in sudden deep thought.

"What is it?" Sally asked.

"I'm just thinking," he said. "How many men has he got over there?"

"I ain't sure," Bradley said. "I'd guess maybe half a dozen."

"Five then after Stout killed that one," Slocum said. "If I was in his place, and I seen what went on here today, I'd be out looking for me some more gun hands."

"Say," Bradley said. "You're right. He'll be trying to hire on some more. We could be moving into a major range war here—and real soon too."

"I may be gone for a few days," Slocum said. "Don't worry about me. I'll be back."

Slocum was out before light the next morning. His saddlebags and blanket roll were packed for an indefinite time on the trail. He hid his big Appaloosa off one side of the road, and he kept himself out of sight too, but from a location where he could watch the Smoot headquarters. It was just after sunup when he saw Tarance come riding away from the ranch house. He watched and waited. Tarance reached the road and turned toward Harleyville. He appeared to be packed as was Slocum, but Slocum could not be absolutely sure of that. The man might just be going into town. He waited long enough to give Tarance a good lead, then mounted up and followed him.

Sure enough, Tarance rode straight through Harleyville without stopping. Slocum kept on his trail. Near noon, Tarance stopped for a cold meal. Slocum, at a distance, did the same. When Tarance moved out again, so did Slocum. He was pretty sure that his thoughts had been correct. Pretty sure that Tarance was out on a trip to recruit gunslingers. Of course, he could be wrong. Perhaps Tarance had quit or been fired and was simply leaving the valley for good, but Slocum did not think so. He kept on the trail. It was late evening before Tarance stopped again. This time he made a camp. He built a fire and cooked himself a meal. He boiled coffee. Slocum did not take a chance by doing the same thing. He did not want to alert Tarance to his presence on the trail. He ate another cold meal and drank water. Then he crawled under his blanket for the night.

He crawled under his blanket, but he did not immediately sleep. He was thinking. He could not recall that Tarance had ever seen him. In fact, Slocum had kept pretty much out of sight after that first day in Harleyville. He and Golden had stopped by Golden's place to meet Smoot and see if Golden could pay rent and move on in his own house. He tried to recall if Tarance had been one of the men on the porch that day. He did not think so. Even if Tarance had been one of the men, that brief meeting might not have been enough for him to recall Slocum. He threw off the blanket and got up. Rummaging through his things in the dark, he found a shirt he had not worn for some time, and he changed into it. Then he dug out a jacket and put it on. He knew that he needed a shave, and it would be even worse by the time he would see Tarance face to face. He packed up, saddled up and rode into the darkness.

Riding wide around Tarance's campsite along the trail, Slocum moved well ahead of the man he had been following. He swung back onto the trail then and looked back. He could see no evidence of Tarance's campfire. He stopped and made his own camp then. He built a fire and made some coffee. He drank a few cups, then settled in for the night.

Slocum opened his eyes the next morning to the sound of approaching hoofs. The sun was well up. He tossed aside his blanket, stood and strapped on his Colt. He waited. Tarance came riding up holding his hands out to the side so as to appear to be friendly. Slocum stood waiting in a stance that indicated the opposite. He looked like a man just waiting for trouble.

"I ain't looking for a fight," Tarance said.

"What are you looking for?"

"I'm just riding through, but I ain't seen no one along this road for a whole day and night. You got some coffee?"

"I got some."

"Would you share a pot with a stranger?"

"Climb on down," Slocum said. "I'll build up the fire."

"I'll go fetch some water," said Tarance.

Slocum noticed the way Tarance was looking at him, and he was pleased with himself. He thought that he had made just the right appearance.

9

Slocum did not think that he was in any real danger from Tarance. Nevertheless, he acted furtive, as if he was wary of someone on his trail. Every move he made, he watched Tarance out of the corner of an eye, and he made his stealth obvious to the other man. He was also careful to keep his right hand mostly unoccupied. These little touches of extra caution did not go unnoticed by Tarance. They sat across the fire from one another waiting for the coffee to boil, and Tarance made a sudden move. Slocum's Colt was out, cocked and aimed at Tarance faster than hummingbird wings.

"Hold it there," said Tarance, raising his hands. "I wasn't going for no gun."

"Sudden moves make me nervous," Slocum said. He held the revolver on Tarance for another tense moment, then eased down the hammer and reholstered the Colt. "I think that coffee's ready now. Help yourself."

Tarance leaned forward for a tin cup. He poured it full and offered it to Slocum. Slocum took it in his left hand, and Tarance poured a second cup for himself.

"You, uh, you got someone on your trail?" Tarance asked.

"If I did," said Slocum, "would I be telling a stranger?"

"I don't mean to be sticking my nose into your business," Tarance said, "but I got me a reason. Let me try it a different way. You looking for a job?"

"I'm broke," said Slocum. "What kind of job you talking about?"

"A job for someone who can pull a six-gun the way you pulled that one on me," Tarance said. "That is, if he ain't a-skeered to go on ahead and pull the trigger."

"I've pulled my trigger more than once."

"I'll bet you have. Well? You interested?"

"Tell me more," said Slocum.

"I work for a man what's expecting some trouble," Tarance said. "We're looking to be ready for it. That's all. I been authorized to hire as many as twelve good men."

"That's a bunch of guns. You looking for a small war?"

"Could be."

"Where is this job?"

Tarance jerked his head to indicate the road behind him.

"Just back down the trail a day's ride or so," he said. "Place called Whistling Valley. The man I work for owns the whole valley, but there's a mess of ranchers squatted on it who disagree."

"Seems like I heard something about that," Slocum said. "Whistling Valley. Yeah. Something about a land grant. Seems like the man's name was Smoot. Something like that."

"That's the man. I work for him. Handling that gun the way you do, you could too. The pay's good. The other side won't be much trouble. They're a bunch of ranchers and cowhands is all. They ain't gunfighters. None of them."

"How many men you got right now?"

"There's five of us."

"You're going out to hire twelve more," Slocum said. "That'll make it seventeen. Sounds to me like you're looking for trouble from somewhere."

"We just mean to be prepared," said Tarance. "That's all."

"Let me get this straight," Slocum said. "Your boss, this, uh—"

"Smoot."

"Yeah. This Smoot. He got hold of an old land grant. How'd he get it?"

"I don't know," Tarance said. "All I know is he got it."

Slocum reached out for the coffeepot in order to refill his

cup. When he had done that, Tarance did the same.

"All right then. He got it," Slocum said. "Then what? He just ride down in the valley and tell all them folks that he owned their land and they got to move?"

Tarance shrugged. "More or less," he said. "He went to court. The court said the land grant's good, and he owns the land."

"Then what's the problem?"

"Some of them ranchers ain't going to abide by the court's decision," Tarance said. "Some of them mean to stay where they are no matter what the court says. We done had a man killed by one of them."

Of course, Slocum knew that the man killed had been rustling Simon Stout's cattle, and Stout had killed him. He knew too that there had been two more men with the rustler. He wondered if maybe this visitor to his camp was one of them.

"Well, what do you say?" said Tarance. "I ain't got all day to set here a-jawing. I got men to hire. I got to get on down the road."

"I don't think so," said Slocum.

"You don't want the job?"

"I don't want the job, and I don't think you need to be getting on down the road."

"What the hell are you talking about?"

"I don't think you need seventeen men to do battle with those ranchers back there."

Tarance put down his coffee cup slowly, keeping his eyes on Slocum.

"That's my business," he said. "None of yours." He stood up. "I'll just be hitting the trail. Thanks for the coffee."

"You can hit the trail," Slocum said, "but ride back the way you came."

"Now look here—"

"You heard me. I ain't going to say it again."

"How come you to go messing in this thing?"

"That's my business and none of yours."

Tarance stood uncertainly. He did not want to take orders from this trail bum, but he had seen him draw that Colt. Should he stand up to this man and take a chance on dying for the sake of his pride?

"If I ride on the way I was going—"

"I'll kill you," Slocum said.

Tarance hung his head. "I'll go back."

"Before you mount up," Slocum said, "drop that gun belt."

Tarance shot Slocum an unbelieving look. Then he unbuckled his belt and let it drop to the ground.

"Back away from it," Slocum said.

As Tarance backed away, Slocum stood up and walked over to pick up the gun belt. Then he walked to Tarance's horse and got the rifle. He moved to his big Appaloosa and mounted up. Carrying both of Tarance's weapons, he rode over beside Tarance's horse and took hold of the reins.

"I'll leave him a ways down the road for you," he said, and he moved out, leaving Tarance standing alone with no horse and no guns.

"Hey," Tarance shouted. "Don't leave me like this. What the hell did I ever do to you anyhow?"

It was already late evening by the time Slocum arrived back at the Ringy Dingy. He was smiling to himself as he moved to the corral, knowing that Tarance was still some miles away from his temporary home at Golden's ranch. He had ridden, he estimated, between two and three miles, probably closer to three, before he turned loose Tarance's horse. The man would have blisters on his feet and a lot of explaining to do. Slocum unsaddled his Appaloosa and turned it into the corral. He walked to the ranch house where he found Golden and Julie sitting quietly in two chairs that were pulled close together.

"Am I interrupting anything?" he said, stepping up onto the porch.

"No. Course not," said Golden. "Pull up a chair."

Julie stood up. "I'll just go in and tell Sally you're back," she said. "She'll want to know."

Slocum sat down and took out a cigar. As he was lighting it up, Golden asked him, "Well? What happened? Where you been?"

Slocum puffed, getting the cigar going well. "Be patient," he said.

Julie came back out of the house, followed by Sally and old Bradley. Julie resumed her seat next to Golden, and Bradley pulled a chair over and sat down.

"I followed that one feller out of there this morning," Slocum said. "He rode right on through Harleyville and kept going. Rode all day. Made himself a camp for the night. I come up with an idea, so I rode wide around him and then set up my own camp and waited. Sure enough, come morning, he come riding right up. Stopped to have coffee with me. He didn't recognize me. Told me he was out to hire gunfighters. A dozen. Offered me a job. Well, I stripped him of his guns and horse and headed back. I dropped his horse off a ways down the road. I figure he's still making his way back."

"You should a stripped him nekkid and kept his horse," Sally said.

"If they try it again," said Slocum, "maybe we'll just do that."

"You think they will try it again?" asked Golden.

"Well, they set out to do it once," Slocum said. "They feel the need for a dozen more gunfighters, they'll try again, I reckon."

"Yeah," Bradley said. "They'll have another go at it all right. Slocum, you done good. We know now what ole Smoot has in his mind to do."

"He's planning for trouble all right," Slocum said. "One way or the other."

"What do you mean?" Julie asked.

"Well, if Grimes wins for you in court," Slocum said, "Smoot ain't giving it up, and if Smoot wins, well, he figures you all ain't going to give it up either."

"Well, he's damn right about that," Bradley said. "Say, I think you earned yourself a drink or two."

Julie stood up. "I'll get it," she said. She went inside.

"I think we'd ought to watch that bunch pretty close from here on," Slocum said. "Next time one of them rides out like that, we need to stop him too. If we can do it, we need to keep Smoot from bringing in more guns."

"I'll set up a schedule with some of the boys," Bradley said.

Just then Julie came back out carrying a tray with a bottle and glasses. She poured drinks all the way around. She even poured one for herself. Bradley drank his down in a gulp and poured himself another.

"Yeah," he said. "If we can keep the bastards bunched up till Grimes gets back with the news, then we'll serve our own papers on them and tell them to get the hell out of the valley, and if they won't budge, why, hell, we'll just blast them out."

Smoot heard the heavy boot steps on the porch. He looked up from behind the desk to see the door open and Tarance came sore-footing into the room, looking bedraggled as hell.

"What're you doing back so soon, and what the hell happened to you?" he demanded.

Tarance hobbled over to the desk and sat down heavily in a chair across the desk from Smoot.

"You ain't going to believe this," he said.

"Try me. What the hell happened?"

"I rode all day yesterday," said Tarance. "Made me a camp for the night. This morning early, I headed out again. I hadn't gone far when I come on a one-man camp. The ranny at the camp appeared to be some nervous, like someone was after him maybe. He looked tough enough too. It come to me that he might be a gunnie on the loose. I stopped to have some coffee with him, and I asked him some questions, you know, to try to feel him out.

"Once I even made a kind of threatening move, and he had his six-shooter out faster'n a greased goose turd. Well, eventually I asked him if he was a-looking for work, and I offered him a job. He turned me down. I got ready to get on my way, and he told me I had to head back the way I come. He said he'd kill me if I went the other way. Then he took my guns and my horse and rode off with them. I had to walk near five miles before I come on where he left my horse. He never left my guns though."

"Who the hell was this man?"

Tarance shook his head.

"If I ever seen him before, I don't recollect it."

"Is he working for the ranchers?"

"I figure he must be."

"Damn it," said Smoot. He reached for a bottle and poured himself a drink, then downed it in a gulp. He poured another.

"I could sure use one a them," Tarance said.

"You sure ain't earned it," said Smoot. "Aw, hell, help yourself."

Tarance poured himself a tall whiskey and took a swallow.

"You can't blame me," he said. "Who'd a ever thought a rangy, bum-looking bastard like that would be greased lightning and would turn on me the way he done? Hell, I found him sitting beside the road a day's ride from here."

"Tarance, we got to have them gunfighters."

"I know that, Boss."

"Especially now. Now that we know the ranchers has got a gunslinger like that."

"I wouldn't face that man, Boss. I seen how fast he is. The only way I could even try to kill the son of a bitch would be a shot in the back. I never seen a man that fast."

Smoot stroked his chin in deep thought.

"I know one man who might could take on a man like that," he said. "And I think I know how to get a hold of him by telegraph wire. We still need them others for the numbers, but we need this man I'm thinking about to take on the one you run into."

"Who you talking about, Boss?"

"I'm talking about P. T. Graves."

"The one they call Gravedigger?"

"That's him."

"You know the Gravedigger?"

"We've met. I think I can get him. He don't come cheap, but there's a hell of a lot at stake here. Listen. Let's you and me go into town tomorrow early, and I'll send that wire."

"All right."

"We still need them others though for the numbers. Maybe we'll send someone else out on that chore tomorrow."

Tarance downed the rest of his whiskey and poured himself another.

"Boss, I been thinking. What if that ranny that held me up

is for a fact working for the ranchers? What if he was on purpose laying for me out there? That'd mean he was a watching the place and seen me ride out."

"You might be right about that."

"If he seen me ride out, he'll see anyone else who tries it. He'll stop us again."

"Yeah."

"Reckon that there Gravedigger would round up some men and bring them along whenever he comes?"

"I don't know," Smoot said. "From what all I know, he works alone. And it might take some up-front cash to get them to come along, and I wouldn't want to ask him to be fronting no cash. Hey. I got it. If I can get Graves out here, then we'll send you out again. You'll ride out just like you done yesterday. We'll let that gunfighter, whoever he is, follow you out, but I'll have Graves to tag along behind. That way, whenever the gunfighter comes at you again, Graves will be there to come up behind him. We'll trap the son of a bitch that way. Grimes will kill him, and you'll already be on your way to round up our gun hands."

"It sounds good except for one thing," Tarance said.

"What's that?"

"We don't know yet if you can get Graves out here."

"That's what we'll find out in the morning," Smoot said. "Here. Have another drink."

"There's another thing I don't like about your plan, Boss."

"Let's hear it."

"I hate to think about facing that man again, even with the Gravedigger just back down the trail. What if he don't get to us in time? I could be killed dead. Then if he comes along and kills the other feller, what the hell difference does that make to me? I'm done dead."

Smoot heaved a sigh of exasperation.

"All right, look here," he said. "If we get Grimes out here, we'll work out a plan with him. We'll figure it to where you'll feel safe enough. Right now, why don't you just put it all out of your mind? Drink up your whiskey and get on to bed. You need a good night's sleep."

Tarance turned the glass up and emptied it. He put the glass on the desk and stood up with a groan. The weight on his much-abused feet was almost more than he could bear.

"What's wrong?" Smoot asked.

"My feet's all blistered up. Real bad."

"Well, soak them before you sleep. Go on now."

Tarance hobbled to the door and went out on the porch. He limped his way down the steps and headed for the bunkhouse, wincing with each painful step. He thought about Slocum, though not by name. He sure would like to have that man at his mercy, maybe with twelve guns aimed at him at once. Better yet, tied to a tree. He wanted to make him suffer, the way he himself was suffering with each step. He did not want to shoot the man in the back. He wanted him to know who was doing it and why, and he wanted it to be slow and painful.

10

The next day Slocum went into Harleyville with Julie, Golden and Sally. Some supplies were needed at the Ringy Dingy, and even though Slocum thought that they would be safe, he decided to ride along just to be sure. If Smoot was trying to hire on more guns, Slocum reasoned, he was feeling insecure, and he wouldn't be likely to start any trouble. So in spite of the fact that he was sort of "riding shotgun," he was fairly relaxed. The ladies went into the general store to do the shopping, and Slocum and Golden went into the saloon for a drink. Smoot was sitting at a table in a far corner with Tarance. Tarance stiffened at the sight of Slocum. He put a hand on Smoot's arm.

"What?" Smoot said.

"That feller there that just come in," Tarance said. "That's him. That's the man that stole my horse and guns."

"The man with Golden?"

"I don't know Golden," said Tarance. "The biggest of them two. The one in the red shirt. He wasn't dressed like that out there on the trail, and he had some whiskers, but that's him. I'd know him anywhere."

"Hell," Smoot said, "I met him. Them two come by the ranch right after we had court here. Well, I guess it was the next day. Golden wanted to know if he could pay rent for his place like the others is doing. I turned him down on accounta I'm using the place. That other feller there, he was with him that day. I told them they oughta just move on out of this territory. I figured they had."

"Well, it sure don't look like they've moved out."

"No, it don't. What the hell was that man's name? I can't recall. I can't even be sure that they said his name. I remember Golden is all, and I remember that son of a bitch there was with him. Damn. I bet they've been here all along."

"Reckon where they're staying?"

"See if you can find out," said Smoot.

"Slocum," said Golden, "I really don't care for the company in here."

"I saw them," Slocum said. "The one with ole Smoot is the one I met up with out on the trail. They've been eyeballing us all right."

"You think they'll try something?"

"He sure didn't want to try me out there on the road," said Slocum. "I doubt if his boss will be any braver."

"Wonder what they're doing in town."

"They might be wondering the same thing about us," Slocum said.

They finished their drinks and left the saloon, walking back over to the store. The ladies were just about done, so in a few more minutes, the wagon was loaded with the supplies. Golden got up on the seat to drive. Julie sat beside him. Slocum mounted his Appaloosa, and Sally climbed on the back of her favorite saddle horse.

"Slocum," Sally said, her voice low. "Ole Murv in the store there said he seen that Smoot go down to the telegraph office early this morning. Reckon what he was up to."

"No good, I'll bet," said Slocum. "Hey, Sammy. Hold up there a minute."

"What for?" Golden asked.

"Never mind," said Slocum. "Just wait here for me. I won't be long."

He turned the Appaloosa and rode down to the telegraph office. Dismounting, he went inside. A little man with a shiny bald head looked up from behind the counter and smiled.

"How may I help you?" he said.

"I want to send a wire," Slocum said. He walked to the counter and reached for a pad of paper that was there handy. He picked up a pencil and turned the pad around. Squinting, he studied the indentations on the paper from the previous note. He couldn't make out the words. "Ah, I can't think just how to word it," he said. "Maybe i'll just take a paper along and study it out. I'll come back when I've figured it out."

He ripped the top sheet off the pad and walked out. Mounting up, he rode back to where Golden and the others waited for him.

"Let's go," he said.

Back at the Ringy Dingy, once the wagon was unloaded, Slocum went into the ranch house. Old man Bradley was at work behind his desk. Slocum walked over and pulled a chair up just opposite Bradley.

"You got a pencil?" he asked.

"Sure," Bradley said, finding one and handing it to Slocum. Slocum placed the sheet of paper from the pad at the telegraph office on the desktop. Then, turning the pencil almost horizontal, he carefully shaded the entire area where the previous writing had left indentations. The words began to emerge.

"What the hell are you doing?" Bradley asked. Sally, Julie and Golden had stepped over to watch over Slocum's shoulder by then.

"Smoot's telegraph message," Slocum said.

"What is it?" asked Sally.

"It's to someone named Graves," Julie said. "It's hard to read like that."

Slocum handed the paper across to Bradley, and Bradley squinted at it.

"Whoever this Graves is," he said, "it looks like Smoot's trying to hire him for something."

"P. T. Graves," Slocum said. "They call him the Gravedigger. He's a gunfighter and a professional killer. I've seen him in action. He's a dangerous man. And he's expensive. I'd say Smoot's getting desperate."

"Well, what'll we do?" asked Golden.

"The wire's already been sent," Slocum said. "What we

don't know is if it's been received on the other end. We don't know if Graves was there to get it, and if he did get it, we don't know if Smoot was able to hire him on. We'll just have to wait and see."

It was early morning and still dark when Art rode out from the Smoot headquarters. Smoot had sent him on the same errand that Tarance had gone on the time Slocum had foiled their purpose. Smoot thought that maybe they wouldn't notice Art. Even if they were watching, he thought that maybe Art would be able to slip by them under cover of darkness.

But Dave Bradley was watching, hidden in almost the same spot where Slocum had watched Tarance ride out. Dave gave Art a head start, then followed him. He followed him into Harleyville and out the other side of town. He stayed on the trail for the rest of the day. He was thinking about something Sally had said, and he did not want to stop Art too soon, too close to Harleyville and the Smoot headquarters. At the end of the long day's ride, he waited while Art set up his camp. Then, leaving his own horse a distance behind, he worked his way quietly to near the camp. Art was busy building up his fire. Dave raised his rifle to his shoulder and fired a shot into the fire. Art jumped to his feet, reaching for his six-gun.

"I wouldn't touch that iron if I was you," Dave hollered.

Art looked around desperately. He couldn't tell where his attacker was located out in the darkness. He held his hands out to his sides, well away from his weapon.

"Don't shoot, mister," he said. "Don't shoot."

"Unbuckle that gun belt and toss it out this way."

Art did as he was told, flinging the gun and gun belt well out into the darkness. Dave looked carefully into the camp. Art's horse was back behind the fire a ways, but it looked as if he had not yet unsaddled the creature. Dave couldn't be sure.

"Is your horse saddled?" he called.

"Yeah," Art said. "I was fixing to—"

"You got a saddle gun on him?"

"Yes, sir."

"Move over to your left."

Art began sidestepping, and Dave moved in toward the

camp. As Art was about to step into darkness, Dave stopped him.

"That's far enough," he said.

Dave stopped. Keeping well out of the light of the fire, Dave walked around and back to Art's horse. He climbed into the saddle.

"Now get out of them clothes," he said.

"What?"

"You heard me. Strip off."

"Wait a minute, mister. You can't—"

Dave fired a round into the ground just in front of Art's feet, and Art jumped straight up and yelped. When he came back down, he started pulling off his shirt as fast as he could. Then he pulled off his boots and his trousers.

"Get out of them socks and long johns too," said Dave.

"You mean—get nekkid?"

"That's what I said."

Soon Art was standing stark naked and trembling. Dave made him walk back over by the fire. Then he rode Art's horse over to the spot where Art had dropped his clothes. He dismounted and gathered them up. Climbing back into the saddle, he took Art's horse, guns and clothes and rode away. When he got back to where he had left his own horse, he gathered up its loose reins and led it along. It was the next morning when he got back to the Ringy Dingy. He turned the horse loose and burned the clothes.

Two days later, Art was lurking in the bushes across the road from the entrance to Sam Golden's ranch, the temporary outlaw headquarters of Smoot. He was waiting for darkness, for he did not want to be seen. He was naked, cut and bruised. His feet were worn raw from the long barefoot walk. He waited until the sun was down, and then cautiously and gingerly made his way across the road. The walk from the gate to the bunkhouse seemed like an eternal walk. He did not think that he could make it. He had been walking and starving for two days, and it seemed as if he would be doing so forever. But the ranch house was in sight.

Art was hoping to make it past the ranch house and on to

the bunkhouse without being seen. If he could do that, then he hoped that no one would be in the bunkhouse when he reached it. That way, he could get in and get some clothes on before anyone saw him. Each step he took was like death. He wondered if his feet would ever be any good for anything again. He wondered if he would lose them entirely. He was picking his way timidly past the big house when he heard someone call out.

"Hey. Who's there?"

The door of the ranch house was flung open, and Smoot came out onto the porch. He was joined there by Tarance, or maybe Tarance had been there already. Maybe Tarance was the one who had hollered out.

"What is it?" Smoot said.

"There's someone over there," said Tarance, pulling out his six-gun.

"Who are you?" Smoot called out. "Speak up or we start shooting."

"Don't shoot," Art said in a quavering voice. "It's me. Art. Let me be. I've got to get over to the bunkhouse."

"What do you mean?" Smoot asked. "What're you doing lurking around like that in the shadders? Where's your horse?"

"Just let me go to the bunkhouse," Art whined. "I'll come back in just a few minutes and tell you all about it."

"You get your ass over here right now," Smoot said, "or I'll tell Tarance here to start shooting."

As Art hobbled toward the porch, he started to cry. As he came into view, the two men on the porch opened their eyes wide in disbelief. Then Tarance started to laugh.

"Shut up," cried Art. "It ain't funny. I'm damn near dead here."

"Yeah," said Smoot. "Shut up. Get in the house and grab a blanket." Tarance went inside still laughing. "Come on over here," Smoot said to Art.

Art crept toward the porch.

"Come on."

"I can't move no faster than this. My feet's all cut up and raw."

"What the hell happened?"

At last Art reached the porch. Tarance stepped out of the house and burst out laughing again. He tossed the blanket to Art who quickly wrapped it around himself and sat down slowly on the edge of the porch. He was still crying.

"What happened?" Smoot said.

"I rode out for a whole day," Art whimpered. "I made a camp. Then someone shot at me from out in the dark. He made me throw out my gun. Then he come in and took my horse. He made me take off my clothes. Then he took my horse, my guns and all my clothes and rode off. He left me like that. It took me all this time to walk back here. I'm starving. I need a drink a water, and I need food, and I need a hot bath to soak in. I probably need a doctor to look at my feet."

"All right. All right," Smoot said. "We'll take care of all that. Tarance, go get him a drink. Now, Art, who the hell was it done this to you?"

"I never seen him," Art said. "He kept in the dark the whole time."

"Damn," said Smoot. "It was likely the same one that jumped Tarance the other day."

"He never done Tarance as bad as he done me," Art whined. "I'm dying here."

Tarance stepped back out onto the porch carrying a bottle and glass. He poured whiskey in the glass and handed it to Art. Art gulped it greedily.

"They're watching us all right," said Smoot. "They know we're wanting to hire on some more guns, and they're watching us real close. They ain't going to let no one get through. Tarance, I want you to get back into town first thing in the morning and see if I've got an answer yet from Graves. We need Graves to take care of that one gunfighter they got over there. We get him, we oughta be able to handle the rest."

"Give me some more whiskey," said Art.

Over at the Ringy Dingy, old man Bradley, Slocum, Dave, Golden, Julie and Sally all sat in chairs on the porch. They had drinks all around. Lefty came riding in from the direction of the road. He walked his horse up to the porch, and he started laughing.

"You'll never guess what I just seen," he said.

"Tell us," Bradley said.

"I was over there watching Smoot's gang, you know. I just got relieved. That's how come I'm back. Anyhow, I was set-ting there a-watching, and I seen that Art come a-sneaking back in the dark. He was nekkid as a jaybird and walking real slow and easy like as if his feet was a-killing him."

Dave burst out laughing then, and the others all joined in. When they finally calmed down a little, Bradley offered Lefty a drink. Lefty got off his horse and walked up to the porch.

"Thank you," he said. "Just one. I need to get me some sleep."

He had a drink, and he talked a little more about how pitiful Art looked, creeping around naked, trying to avoid being seen, flinching and wincing with each tiny step he took. They all laughed more at every word. Finally Lefty took his leave and headed for the corral to take care of his horse.

"Reckon who they'll send out next," said Golden.

"When they seen how that Art looked when he come back," Sally said, "they won't likely be able to talk no one else into trying it."

They laughed some more.

"You know," said Dave, "it was Sally that give me that idea."

"I did suggest that, didn't I?" she said.

They had another round of drinks, and then Sally stood up.

"I'm going to ride over to my place," she said. "There's some things over there I need to take care of."

"Won't they wait till morning?" Julie asked.

"I been thinking about them all day," said Sally. "I can't let them go no longer."

"Well, you can't be riding out like that by yourself after dark," Bradley said.

Slocum stood up.

"I'll go along with her," he said.

"Well, all right," said Bradley. "If she insists on going. We won't argue no more."

"You don't have to go," Sally said to Slocum. "Hell, I can take care of myself."

"I got nothing else to do," Slocum said.

"Well, come on then."

They stepped down off the porch and started walking toward the corral. For a while neither said anything. Close to the corral and out of earshot of those back on the porch, Sally said, "I was hoping you'd say that."

"Say what?"

"That you'd come along with me," she said. She glanced over at Slocum, and even in the darkness, he could see her wink.

"Well," he said, "I couldn't be sure,'cause I ain't no mind reader, but I kinda had me an idea what you might be up to. I thought I'd better tag along just in case I was right about that."

"Well, let's get saddled up and get on over there," she said. "Time's a wasting."

As Sally and Slocum rode by the porch headed for the gate, the others watched them.

"I wonder what she had to do that was so urgent," Julie said. "I hope they'll be all right."

"Slocum can take care of the both of them," Golden said.

"I reckon she had some holes that needed to be plugged," said Dave.

Old Bradley kicked Dave in the leg, and Dave hollered.

"What?" Julie asked.

"He didn't say nothing," Bradley said. "Never mind."

Julie looked at Golden.

"What'd he say?"

"I don't know," said Golden. "It didn't make no sense to me."

11

In the middle of the bunkhouse floor on what should have been Sam Golden's ranch, Art lounged in a tub filled with hot, sudsy water. His wretched-looking feet were sticking out of the water, resting on the edge of the tub. He held a bowl of stew in one hand, and with the other he was shoveling spoonfuls of the thick broth and chunks of meat and potatoes into his mouth. A platter of biscuits, a glass and a whiskey bottle were on a table just beside the tub. Tarance came walking into the bunkhouse.

"Don't say nothing to me," Art said.

"I just come to apologize for laughing at you," said Tarance.

Art stopped shoveling and looked at Tarance suspiciously.

"You mean that?"

"I mean it, Art. Hell. I wasn't thinking. I got to remembering how I felt whenever I had to walk back, and I had all my clothes and my boots. I had my horse too after only a few miles. I guess what he done to you was pretty damn bad."

"Bad ain't the word for it. I don't know no word to describe it. It was awful. It was horrible. It was worse than all that. I don't know no word for it."

"Art, you reckon it was that same gunfighting son of a bitch that got me?"

"I told you, I never seen the man."

"You said he come on you at night?"

"That's right."

"He was out ahead of me in the morning. He let me come on him. He took a shot at you without no warning?"

"Right outa the dark. That's right."

"You know what, Art?"

"What?"

"I don't think it was the same man. It's a whole different style. I bet you that they got different ones a-watching us. On shifts. That's what I think."

"Sons of bitches," Art said. He stuck another spoonful of stew in his mouth.

"Smoot says we shouldn't do nothing just yet," said Tarance. "He says wait for the Gravedigger to get here. Hell, we don't even know if the Gravedigger's coming. I say we oughta start in to getting even. We oughta look for a chance to pick off one or two of them. What do you think?"

"Well, I can't do it," Art said. "The shape I'm in. I can't do nothing for a while yet. But I'll say this. If you go to shooting at them, shoot a few for me. Will you?"

"I promise you that," Tarance said.

Slocum stepped into Sally's ranch house and struck a match. Sally put her hand on his and blew it out.

"I know ever' inch of this place," she said. "We don't need no light. Come on."

Still holding his hand, she led him across the room to the bed. Then she reached a hand behind his head, pulling his head down to meet hers. She kissed him, a long, lingering, wet and passionate kiss. Finally coming up for air, she backed off and started pulling off her shirt.

"I don't want to waste no time," she said.

Slocum pulled off his own shirt and sat down on the edge of the bed to take off his boots.

"Take it easy, Sally," he said. "I'm not going nowhere without you. Not tonight anyhow."

When Slocum stood up again to unfasten his jeans, Sally was already naked. She reached to help him out of the rest of his clothes. As soon as he was completely undressed, standing there in front of her, she reached out to take hold of his cock. In anticipation of things to come, it had already come to attention. She gripped it hard, and it bucked and throbbed in her hand. She moved her naked body in close to his, pressing herself against him, and their lips met again in another passionate kiss. Slowly, Sally sank to her knees, her tongue trailing down his chest and stomach as she did.

Darting out her tongue, she teased his cock head, licking it all around. Then she licked lower, balancing his heavy balls on her tongue. At last she sucked in his full length, moving her head back and forth, and in response, he began thrusting, fucking her face. She slurped greedily. At last, he spurted, again and again, and she swallowed it down. When he was all done, they lay down together on the bed and cuddled and kissed, stroking each other's bare bodies.

After a few quiet minutes, she reached again for his tool, and, stroking it gently, she brought it back to life. He moved on top of her as she opened her legs to accept him. She reached down to take hold of his cock and guide it into her warm, wet, waiting hole. He slipped in easily, pushing deep, going in all the way. They had a nice, quiet fuck for a little while, but then they began thrusting and humping harder and faster. Soon they were wild in their lust for one another. Slocum drove down hard, and she in turn pounded her pelvis upward against his.

"Ah, fuck me," she said. "Fuck me."

When she came, it was ferocious, and in the middle of her thrashing about, Slocum felt his own release coming. He exploded into her depths, filling her with his hot juices. At last they lay still again, breathing heavily into one another's ears.

"Hey," she said, "if we take a little break, maybe have a drink or two, you think we could do that again?"

"We can damn sure give it a try," he said.

Simon Stout was riding herd. It was a big herd, the combined herds of all the valley's ranchers. He knew that old Bradley had invited them all in saying that he had plenty of grass and plenty of water, but Stout was wondering if it would all hold up until the trouble was over and it was time for the roundup and drive to market. He hoped that it would. In the meantime, all he and the others could do was help keep an eye on things, help hold everything together.

*   *   *

Across the fence, Tarance dismounted, taking his rifle with him. He knew that the gate was being watched in case any of them tried to ride out to go look for new hands, so he had not left the ranch. He had instead ridden to the pasture back behind the ranch house. He hadn't been back there for a while, not since the last time he and Ned and Art had driven stolen cows back there, and he was curious about how quiet it was. He had not come across any of the stolen cattle. He decided to look around later. Right now he had other business to attend to. Kneeling behind a fence post, he squinted his eyes toward the lowing cattle on the other side. At last he spotted a rider, a lone rider.

Tarance cranked a round into the chamber of his rifle and raised the rifle to his shoulder. It took a little while to focus on his target in the dark, but he at last managed to get the rider just on top of the front sight. He took a deep breath and let it out slowly, squeezing the trigger. The roar of the rifle shattered the stillness of the dark night, and Simon Stout fell dead with a bullet in his back.

It was near sunrise when Dave Bradley rode out to relieve Stout at the herd. The first thing he noticed wrong was Stout's riderless horse. He considered that Stout might have dismounted for some legitimate reason. He rode around looking and calling Stout's name. Then he came across the body.

"The shot had to have come across the fence from over there where Smoot and his men are at," Dave was telling his father. "It couldn't have come from nowhere else."

"Why would they resort to murder at this point?" Bradley said.

"They were looking to hire gunfighters," said Slocum. "Maybe they're just trying another way of evening up the odds."

"Well, I say we get together and ride them down," said Dave.

"That could be just what they're trying to get us to do," Slocum said.

"You mean they might have an ambush laid for us?" Bradley asked.

"Could be."

"Ambush or not, I say let's get to killing," Dave said. "They shot poor ole Simon in the back. He never even had a chance."

"I know, son," Bradley said, "and I know how you feel. I feel the same way. But let's think on it for a spell. Grimes will be getting back real soon now. Let's see what he has to tell us. Then we'll make our plans."

It seemed as if everyone on both sides of the Whistling Valley controversy had gone into Harleyville to wait for the stage to come in from the capital. Lawyer Grimes was due to be on it, and he should be bringing word about the filing of the papers and the stay against Smoot. Slocum looked across the street at Smoot, flanked by his gunmen, and he thought that Smoot had a particularly smug look on his face. The man must have something up his sleeve, he thought, or he knows something we don't know.

Then the stage came rolling into town. People crowded around. It came to a rocking and dusty stop, and both doors were flung open. A middle-aged woman got out. A man with the look of an eastern drummer followed. A preacher and a cowhand were the last two to disembark. Bradley looked at Slocum. Slocum shrugged. Bradley strode over to the stage and looked at the driver who was just coming down from his high perch.

"Stormy," Bradley said. "Where's Grimes?"

"Who?"

"You know, damn it. We've all been waiting for him for two weeks now. Lawyer Grimes."

"Oh, him. He never got on the stage. I ain't seen him since—Hey. Wait a minute. I weren't driving that day he went over to the capital, so I near forgot. Hell, I'm forgetting things all the time these days. The day he headed over there, someone stopped the stage. Masked man. He didn't take nothing. Nothing except for Grimes. Made him get off and then told the driver to get on, and he did. Left them both standing in the road."

"Both alive?"

"Last he seen them."

"Damn it, Stormy, that was two weeks ago. Why weren't we told about it before now?"

Stormy shook his head.

"It were reported to the law over at the capital," he said. "That's all I know."

Bradley turned to Slocum.

"Did you hear all that?"

"I heard it," said Slocum. "There's a whole lot more going on here than we ever thought."

"I'm going to the capital myself," Bradley said.

"Don't say that out too loud," said Slocum. "I'll go with you, but let's keep it quiet."

Back at the Ringy Dingy, Bradley called Dave, Golden, Sally and Julie in to hear his decision. He and Slocum would be riding to the capital first thing in the morning to find out just what the hell was going on.

"I oughta go along," Dave said. "What if you run into trouble?"

"I think we can handle any trouble we run into," Bradley said. "I don't want to leave this place and all these people vulnerable to attack from Smoot. I want you to stay here and keep an eye on things. And don't go starting no range war till we get back. You hear me?"

"I won't start nothing," Dave said, "but if they shoot first—"

"Then you shoot back and kill the bastards," Bradley said.

Tarance was walking from the corral toward the ranch house when another of Smoot's hired men, Scarface Mike, stopped him.

"What is it, Scarface?" asked Tarance.

"Back there in town," Scarface said, "I was kinda hanging around the stage, you know, over on the other side from where old man Bradley was at, and I heard him tell that other feller— he called him Slocum—I heard him say he was going to the capital himself, and then that Slocum, he said, I'll go with you."

"Come on," Tarance said. "Tell it to Smoot."

They walked on over to the ranch house and went inside. Smoot was lounging with a cigar and a glass of whiskey.

"What?" he said.

"Scarface here heard something in town you oughta know about," said Tarance.

"Well, then, what is it?"

"Old man Bradley and that Slocum are going to the capital in the morning," said Scarface.

Smoot stood up and paced, puffing his cigar all the time.

"I was afraid of that," he said.

"Scarface is damn good with a rifle," said Tarance.

"Can you take care of them?" Smoot asked Scarface.

"Sure I can."

"Tarance says that Slocum is deadly fast with a six-gun."

"I won't get close enough to them for him to use no six-gun."

"All right then. See to it."

It was nearly noon the next day when Slocum glanced back over his shoulder. The movement did not escape the notice of old Bradley.

"What is it?" he asked.

"Someone's behind us," said Slocum. "Let's stop and make a camp. Right up there in those trees is a good spot."

"That don't look like no good camp spot to me," Bradley said.

"It is for what I have in mind," said Slocum.

They rode easy, and when they reached the trees, they rode in under them and dismounted. Slocum quickly gathered some sticks and built a small fire. They unsaddled their horses. Slocum pulled an extra shirt out of his blanket roll. Gathering leaves and grass, he stuffed it full and propped in up against his saddle. Then he perched his hat on top of it.

"Let me have your jacket," he said to Bradley.

He did the same thing with Bradley's jacket and hat. From a distance, it would appear that the two men were sitting across the fire from one another. Then Slocum and Bradley took their rifles and moved behind some trees. They waited.

*   *   *

Scarface saw the two men ride into the small patch of woods. A moment later he saw a small wisp of smoke. He knew that they had stopped to camp, probably have a noon meal. Well, he thought, that would save him the fixing of a meal. He would just kill them and eat their food. He hoped they had something besides beans. He hoped that they were making coffee too. Riding easy, he studied the lay of the land ahead. Across from the camp in the clump of trees was a hillside, rocky and brush covered. Scarface did not want to alert his intended victims. He had no intention of getting into a gunfight. All he wanted was a good line of fire and two quick shots without warning.

He moved off the road and swung a wide arc, eventually coming up on the far side of the hill he had already selected. At the base of the hill, he dismounted and tied his horse. Taking his rifle, he climbed the hill. He was puffing a little by the time he reached the top, for he was used to riding everywhere he went. Still, he moved in a crouch. He skulked across the top of the hill to the other side and peeked cautiously over to the clump of trees on the other side of the road down below. He saw the smoke first. He went a little down the hillside and settled in behind a large boulder. He checked his sight lines to the fire.

Then he saw the two figures sitting at the fire. It would be easy. He chambered a shell and scooted around some, getting just the right position for both comfort and a good shot. He raised the rifle to his shoulder and took careful aim. At that distance, he couldn't tell who was who, so he decided to take the one facing him first. To reach, the other would have to turn around to look for his attacker. Scarface was sure that he could take them both before the second one could react. He squeezed off the first shot, saw a puff come out of the chest of the first target, quickly chambered a second round, re-aimed, fired again, and saw the telltale puff come from the back of the second target.

He straightened up and looked hard. Both men had been hit. He knew that. Neither had fallen though. Both just sort of slumped. Well, he thought, stranger things had happened. They were sitting up dead, both of them. He stood up, chambered another round just in case, and went back down the back side of the hill to his horse. Mounting up, he rode around the hill, across the road and on up to the camp. The "dead men" had not moved. They did not move as he rode closer in. He stopped. He squinted. Something was wrong.

Then it came to him like a revelation an instant too late. They were dummies. He had fallen into a trap. His brain told him to turn and run, but his body had not responded to the call when Slocum spoke from behind a tree.

"Throw down the rifle," he said.

Instead, Scarface raised the rifle. It was his last mistake. Slocum fired his Colt from behind the tree, and the lead smashed into Scarface's nose and upward through his brain. Blood and brains flew out the back of his head. His arms jerked and tossed the rifle. The body twitched in the saddle, and the head bobbed foolishly on the shoulders. Then what had been Scarface slipped quietly from the saddle and smashed lifelessly to the ground.

Slocum holstered his Colt. He stepped out from behind the tree and looked down at the would-be killer. Bradley came out of hiding to stand beside Slocum.

"I don't think we'll be bothered again," Slocum said.

"Not by that one for sure," said Bradley. "Let's get on the way."

12

It was late evening when Slocum and Bradley arrived at the capital. They had no more trouble along the way. It was too late in the day to take care of any business, so they went to a hotel, but they found that it had no vacancies. They tried two more before they were able to get a room for the night. The capital was crowded. Slocum asked Bradley what was going on, but Bradley said that it was always like that. It was just a busy place. Slocum couldn't imagine how so many people could have business in that place. He was glad of his own lifestyle. He had no business except to find a job now and then to get some money in his jeans.

When they had finally gotten themselves a room, they went to the nearest stable to take care of their horses. They stopped off at a crowded restaurant for an evening meal. It was good, but it was expensive. After an extra cup of coffee, because it was still too early for bed, they went to a saloon. It too was crowded, so they bellied up to the bar to have their whiskeys. Slocum thought that he would be glad when they had taken care of business and were headed back to the ranch. He was uncomfortable around so many people. After a couple of drinks, they went to the hotel and called it a night.

In the morning, they were up early, anxious to get on with it. They had breakfast and walked to the courthouse. Slocum waited outside while Bradley went in. In a few minutes, Bradley came out again. He was in a hurry.

"What'd you find out?" Slocum asked him.

Bradley didn't answer. He lead Slocum to another office and went in there. When he came out, he went to a third. Slocum was losing his patience. Bradley came out of the third office and stopped there beside Slocum. It was the first time he had slowed down. He heaved a sigh.

"There's just one thing left to do," he said. "We go straight to the governor."

"You want to tell me what's going on?" Slocum asked.

"Well, of course, we know that Grimes never got here to file papers," Bradley said. "What I know now is that if he had got here, he'd have found out that there ain't no papers to be filed."

"What do you mean?"

"It seems that Smoot's so-called land grant was never presented nowhere in this city. It seems that the judge that held that hearing over in Harleyville was a God-damned phony. There never was no such judge. Smoot's whole thing is a big fraud. A swindle. And we bought it. There ain't no land grant. There wasn't no hearing. There wasn't no judge's ruling."

"So why do we need to see the governor?" Slocum asked.

"Long as we're here," said Bradley, "I mean to tell him the tale and ask for U.S. marshals to ride over and take care of Smoot and them. If we go after them, some of our boys is liable to get hurt, so why not let the law do its job?"

Slocum shrugged.

"That makes sense," he said.

At the governor's office, Bradley was told that the governor would not be available until after lunch. Bradley and Slocum had a couple of hours to kill. They went to lunch early so they could find a table, and they drank coffee until they were ready to order their lunch.

"That damn Smoot," Slocum said. "He's sitting over there on Sammy's ranch."

"And he's run a couple of people offa theirs," said Bradley. "Not to mention running ever'one who's left over onto my place temporarily."

"He's stole cattle and done some killings," Slocum said. "If that don't bring a marshal, I don't know what it would take."

"We'll take that marshal back with us," Bradley said, "and if he needs any help rounding up that bunch, we'll back him up with all the men he wants, men and guns."

"We can do that all right," Slocum agreed. "You reckon it's about time for us to order up some food?"

"Yeah. I want to get over there as soon as the damn governor is available." Bradley waved his arm at the waiter.

Slocum went into the governor's office with Bradley. They had to go over the whole story twice. At last the governor had it all straight in his head, and he sent for his chief marshal, Dan "Road" Agent. Slocum fidgeted the few minutes they were waiting for Agent to appear. When he arrived, he was wearing a black three-piece suit. The coat was hanging open to show the badge pinned to his vest. He had a flat-brimmed black hat on his head, which he took off as he stepped into the office. He sported a handlebar mustache, and he was wearing two Colts, low and strapped to his thighs.

"You sent for me, Governor?" he said.

"That's right, Road," the governor said. "I want you to meet Mr. Bradley here and Mr. Slocum. Gentlemen, this is United States Marshal Dan Agent. We call him 'Road.' "

Agent shook hands with Bradley and Slocum. Then he pulled up a chair and sat down. The governor summarized Bradley's tale to Agent.

"So he's not only perpetrated a fraud on a whole bunch of innocent, hard-working ranchers," he said, "but he's rustled cattle and killed at least two people, maybe more, and one of them a lawman. Road, I want you to ride back to Whistling Valley with these men and take care of that Smoot and his gang. Do you have any deputies you can take with you?"

"I won't have any available for another week at least," Agent said.

"We can't wait that long," the governor said. "If you need any help, you can temporarily deputize some of Bradley's men. Slocum here maybe."

Slocum winced at the thought. He had worn a badge on

occasion—temporarily—but he had always found it somewhat distasteful.

"All right, Governor," Agent said. He looked at Bradley and Slocum. "When will you two be ready to ride?"

"Just as soon as we can saddle our horses and settle our hotel bill," Bradley said.

"Where are you staying?"

"Place called the Johnson House."

"I'll meet you in front of the hotel," the marshal said, and he left the office.

Bradley thanked the governor for his help, and he and Slocum headed for the stable. They saddled their horses and rode to the hotel. Inside, they packed up their blanket rolls and saddlebags. Bradley paid the bill. When they went back out to their horses, Agent was there, sitting in his saddle waiting for them. They mounted up and rode out of town.

Along the way, Agent asked more questions about the situation in Whistling Valley. He wanted more detail on Smoot's setup, how many men he had, where he was situated. The other two men answered him as best they could. They also told him how Scarface had attempted to kill them along the way and how Slocum had gotten him instead.

"That'll all have to go in the report," Agent said.

Before the sun was too low in the evening sky, they stopped to make camp for the night. They built a small fire and cooked up a trail meal, boiled some coffee and ate. When they finished their meal, they sat around the fire drinking coffee.

"From what you've told me," Agent said, "I don't think I'll have any trouble with this bunch. This Smoot's only got four or five men left. You've already taken out a couple of them. Right?"

"That's right," said Bradley. "But—"

"Hell, down in El Paso last year, I took on the whole Harkey gang single-handed. There were six of them. All six were blasting away at me at the same time, and I killed them all. All I got from it was a little nick on my right arm."

"I heard about that," Slocum said.

"And then up in Montana that time," Agent went on, "I found myself facing eight of the Dunhams."

"They were a tough bunch all right," Slocum said. "I knew them."

"Well, it wasn't a face to face fight in the street like I had with the Harkeys," Agent said. "I dropped down behind a water trough, and they each took cover at different spots along the street. I got a couple of them from there. Then the rest started running between buildings, and I had to chase them down one at a time. Ole Spot Dunham climbed up on the roof of the general store and tried to pick me off from there, but I got him instead. It was quite a fight. I came out of that one without a scratch."

"Slocum," Bradley said, "I'm feeling better already."

"It still might be a good thing," Slocum said, "if you was to follow the governor's advice and deputize a couple of fellers to go along with you—just to play it safe."

Agent shook his head.

"I won't need any help," he said. "Not for a handful of land swindlers."

Smoot was pacing the floor when Tarance stepped into the room from outside. Smoot whirled to face him.

"It's about damn time," he said. "Where the hell have you been? Do you know how long Scarface has been gone? He shoulda been back here yesterday. Something's gone wrong. He didn't get the job done, or else he'd be back already. That means that Bradley's made it to the capital. He knows ever'thing by now. They're going to come down on us with all they've got, and we ain't no match for them. Not now."

"You through now, Boss?"

"What the hell do you mean am I through? I ain't even got started. We got to come up with something quick. Unless we come up with something, we're through here. We might just as well grab what little cash we've gathered up and get the hell out while the getting's good."

"I might just have that something you mentioned," said Tarance. "Someone out here on the porch waiting to meet you."

"What? Who? Who is it?"

"You wanta step out on the porch, or you want me to bring him in?"

"Bring him on in," Smoot said.

Tarance stepped to the door and shoved it open. He leaned his head out and said something, then stepped back in and out of the way. A tall, slender man dressed all in black stepped through the doorway. He wore two six-guns low on his hips and tied down. He had on a flat-brimmed black hat, and he wore a droopy mustache.

"This here's the boss," Tarance said. "Boss, meet the Grave-digger."

Smoot's eyes opened wide and his jaw dropped in astonishment. He stood still for a moment, then rushed to pump Graves's hand.

"Welcome," he said. "Welcome. You came just in the nick of time. Things were just about to get desperate here. Oh, Mr. Graves, you are a sight for sore eyes. Come in and sit down, please. Can I get you a drink? Have a cigar?"

"A cup of coffee," Graves said.

"Yeah. Sure. Coming right up. Tarance, fetch a cup of coffee for our guest."

Tarance left the room, and the Gravedigger sat in the nearest chair. His movements were quick and calculated, almost jerky. Seated, he took the hat off his head and dropped it to the floor beside the chair. His elbows on the arms of the chair, he touched the tips of his fingers together in front of his chest and stared over them at Smoot.

Smoot rushed over behind the desk and opened a drawer. He pulled out a stack of bills and counted some off. Then he walked across the room to where Graves was sitting and held the bills out toward him.

"I know you always get an advance," he said. "Will this cover it?"

Graves took the bills and, without bothering to count them, stuffed them into a shirt pocket.

"It'll do for now," he said.

Tarance came back into the room and handed a cup of steaming coffee to Graves. Graves sipped at it and placed the cup on the table beside the chair.

"What do you want me to do?" he said.

"Well, now," said Smoot, beginning to pace again, "the situation here has changed a bit. Still, the main thing is that gunfighter they've got over there."

"What's his name?"

"Slocum," said Tarance. "I've seen his draw. He's fast."

"I know Slocum," the Gravedigger said. "He's good, but I can take him. You said the main thing. What else is there?"

"I'm thinking that we need to get our hands on the deeds to all the farms," said Smoot. "The land grant has been exposed. It won't do. I need the actual deeds. The owners ain't going to just hand them over. And we need to get them recorded at the land office in town in my name."

"That can all be done," Graves said.

"I'm thinking of something else, Boss," Tarance said.

"What's that?"

"Bradley could be bringing the law back with him."

"Who's this Bradley?" asked Graves.

"The biggest rancher in the valley," said Smoot. "He's the one hired that Slocum."

"Where's he been?"

"He went up to the capital city."

"Then if he brings the law back with him, it'll be U.S. marshals," said Graves.

"Is that a problem?" Smoot asked.

"Not for me. They kill just like anyone else. It could be a problem for you on down the line. How you going to explain it when they send some more down here to check up on things?"

"I'm not worried about that," Smoot said. "If you can handle Slocum and any lawmen that Bradley brings in here, I'll get my hands on all those deeds, and I'll own the whole valley. I'll be rich, and that means I'll be powerful. Lawmen and politicians always listen to the rich and powerful. I'll come up with some story to blame all the killings on Bradley. It'll work. Yeah. It'll work."

"So where do I find Slocum?" asked Graves.

"He went to the capital with Bradley," Tarance said. "We got no way a knowing just when they'd be coming back."

"No sense in chasing around after him. I'll just wait till he's back," said Graves. "In the meantime, I'd like a good steak dinner and a nice hot bath."

"Tarance," said Bradley, "see that Mr. Graves has everything he needs."

"I wish Daddy'd get back," Julie said. She was standing on the front porch of the ranch house on the Ringy Dingy with Sam Golden beside her.

"Don't worry, Julie," Golden said. "Slocum can take care of anything that Smoot bunch might throw at them. Your daddy's safe with Slocum along. You can be sure of that."

She turned to face him and looked up into his eyes.

"Oh, I know you're probably right about that," she said. "It's not that I don't trust Slocum to take good care of Daddy. It's just—well, with everything that's been going on around here, I'll feel much better when I see him home safe and sound."

"I understand," Golden said. He lifted his hands to place them on her shoulder, but she moved in close just then, laying her head on his shoulder and pressing herself against him. He lifted his hands awkwardly, as if he had no idea what to do with them. Then he put his arms around her and held her tight.

"I'm glad you're here," she said.

"I am too."

"I hope everything works out. Will you stay on for good if everything works out?"

"If I actually get possession of my ranch," Golden said, "I mean to stay and make a go of it. I—well, yeah. I mean to stay."

"I'd like that," she said. "Sammy? How do you feel about me? I mean, really."

"Why, I—I admire you a whole lot," he said.

"Is that all? Do you even like me?"

"Oh, yes. I do. I really and truly do like you a whole lot."

"You admire me a whole lot and you like me a whole lot. Sammy, is that all you can say?"

"Well, Julie," he said, "to tell you the truth, there's more things I'd like to say to you. I really would. It just seems to

me that the way things are, I ain't got the right. Why, if anything was to go wrong with this Smoot business, and if I don't
never get to take possession of my ranch over there, well, I
ain't got nothing. I'm just a drifter, a saddle bum. That's all.
But when this is all over, if it all works out for the good, well,
then I'll have some things to say to you."

"I don't want to wait for that time," Julie said. "I need to
hear them right now. Now while we're holding each other
close. Tell me, Sammy. Tell me."

"All right, Julie, if you say so. Julie I—I love you. I love
you more than anything. And when the trouble is over with
and everything's all okay, I'll be asking you to marry up with
me. Julie?"

"Yes?"

"If I was to ask you that question, I mean, when the time's
right, you know, what do you think you'd say?"

"If you asked me that question right now," she said, "my
answer would be yes. And you know why? Because I love
you too, Sam. Did you hear me? I love you."

"Oh, yes," he said. "I heard you. I heard you fine. It just
kinda took my breath away. There was never anything I
wanted to hear more, and I never heard anything in my whole
life that made me as happy as hearing you say them words to
me."

13

B. J. Sim unlocked the door of the land office in Harleyville.
It was precisely eight o'clock in the morning. B. J. Sim was a
prompt and precise man. Only about five feet six inches tall,
Sim was nearing fifty and was beginning to lose his hair. What
he had was slicked back on his head. He wore a thin mustache
and little round spectacles. Though not obese, he did have a
little round potbelly that had developed in only the last four
or five years. As Sim opened the door, Tarance and another
Smoot man shoved their way in behind him. The Gravedigger
followed slowly and deliberately.

"What is this?" said Sim. "Take it easy, gentlemen. I'll be
right with you."

"We're in a hurry," said Tarance.

Graves leaned casually against the front wall of the office,
smoking a thin cigarette and watching with cold, intent eyes.
Sim sought refuge behind his desk.

"Just what is it you want?" he said.

"We work for Mr. Smoot," Tarance said. "You know he has
a land grant for all of Whistling Valley. Just to firm up his
claim, he's in the process right now of getting all the deeds to
all the individual ranches from the former so-called owners.
He sent us down here to have you record all those deeds in
his name."

"I can't change the records without having the signed deeds
in front of me," Sim said.

112 · JAKE LOGAN

"The deeds are being signed," Tarance said. "But like I told you, we're in a hurry. Besides, the deeds are just an extra thing. Smoot already has the land grant, and the court has already upheld it. You know that. Now get busy and change the records here."

"I know about the hearing, of course," said Sim, "but I also know that there's an appeal planned. The court held that Mr. Smoot's land grant is valid, but it did not go the next step and order me to change the records. Until I receive that court order, or until I see the signed deeds, there's nothing I can do."

"Listen here, you little shit—"

"Hold on," said Graves. He walked slowly over to the desk to stand just across from Sim. He stared coldly into Sim's eyes. Tarance and the other Smoot man stepped aside. Suddenly Graves's right-hand Colt was out and cocked and pointed right between Sim's eyes. A small, frightened noise escaped involuntarily from between Sim's lips. "I think there's plenty you can do," said Graves, "if you just make up your mind to do it. And there's plenty I can do if you decide to be stubborn."

Sim leaned forward and to one side to reach under his desk. Graves shoved the Colt closer to the little man's face.

"The—the record book," Sim stammered. "It's right down here."

"Go on then," the Gravedigger said.

Sim pulled the big, heavy book out and laid it on his desk. He opened it up to the Whistling Valley pages. Dipping his quill into the ink bottle on his desk, he began to write. Graves holstered his Colt and looked at Tarance.

"Keep an eye on him," he said. He walked back across the room to lean against the wall where he had been before. The front door was opened, and a man with the look of a farmer stepped inside. "Come back later, friend," Graves said. "There's a major transaction taking place here. It'll take a spell to get done."

"But I—"

"Later."

The farmer looked at Graves and noted the cold, hard eyes and the two low-tied Colts.

"Yes, sir," he said, and he left the office.

*   *   *

Bradley, Slocum and Agent had thought they might make it in to the Ringy Dingy the night before, but after riding a few miles in near-total darkness, they decided that they really should camp the rest of the night and get an early start in the morning. They made it on in by somewhere around ten the next day. The sun was bright, and the day promised to be a warm one. They rode right up to the porch of the ranch house. Lefty was there to greet them and take care of the horses. The three travelers went on in the house. Julie ran to hug her father. When she broke her embrace, Bradley introduced her to Agent.

"Can I fix you all some breakfast?" she asked.

"We did leave in a hurry this morning," Bradley said. "Didn't take time to eat. Didn't even have coffee."

"I'll take care of that right away," she said, and she hurried into the kitchen.

Just then Sally stepped out of a back bedroom.

"Slocum," she said. "Mr. Bradley. Glad to have you back."

"Sally," Slocum said, "this here is Marshal Dan Agent."

Agent took off his hat. "United States marshal, ma'am," he said.

Sally looked from Agent to Slocum to Bradley, anxious curiosity written all over her face.

"We're getting us some feed," Bradley said. "Then we have a tale to tell. We'll need Sammy and Dave and all the other ranch owners to gather up in here in just about an hour. An hour at the most."

"Well, I'll see to that," Sally said. "I'll go spread the word right now."

When the breakfast was done and the ranchers were gathered, Bradley stood up in front of them all.

"My friends," he said, "I have good news for us all. First, I want to introduce to all of you United States Marshal Dan Agent."

"Road Agent?" someone asked.

"That what some call me," Agent said.

"Now here's what we found out at the capital," Bradley continued. "There ain't no damn land grant. The hearing we had in Harleyville was a fake. The judge was a fake, a crony of Smoot's. He's disappeared. Grimes never made it to the capital. He was kidnapped off the stage before it ever got there. Likely he was murdered by Smoot's men. The whole thing is nothing but a well-planned fraud on us all. The governor sent Marshal Agent here to arrest Smoot and his whole gang, and that's all there is to it. That's the whole story."

"You mean we paid him rent on our own places for nothing?"

"That's right."

"When you going to arrest them?"

"Right now," Agent said.

"Let us go along, and we'll just hang them all."

"We can't have that," said Agent. "I'm going alone. I'll round them all up and hold them in the jail in Harleyville till we're sure we have the whole gang. Then I'll transport them to the capital. They'll get a trial."

"Then they'll hang," someone shouted, and they all laughed.

When the laughter died down, someone else said, "Well, I guess that means we can all go on back home."

"What about the cattle?"

"It's near enough time for the roundup and the drive," Bradley said. "You're welcome to leave them here."

"It'll save work later."

"You can all feel free to ride in here and check on your own critters anytime between now and when we drive them out," Bradley said.

"I'm going home."

"Me too."

"What a relief to have that all over with."

"It was all a fraud—right from the start."

The crowd was moving out, and Julie found her way to Golden's side.

"Well, Sammy," she said, "it won't be long now. You'll get to move onto your own ranch."

He put an arm around her shoulders.

"Will you marry me?" he said.

"Yes," she said. "I will. Let's tell Daddy."

"And Slocum," Golden said. "And Sally. Hell, let's tell the whole world."

With all the celebrating, no one seemed to notice as Marshal Agent left the room, no one, that is, except Slocum. Slocum wished that Agent hadn't been so stubborn. Things just didn't feel right. He thought the celebrating was all a bit premature. Smoot was still ensconced in Sammy Golden's ranch house. He had four or five men over there with him, and in spite of Agent's bragging tales, he was only one man. Smoot had already killed a lawman. He wouldn't hesitate to kill another. Then there was the matter of the telegram to Graves. Even with Smoot's scheme finally exposed as a fraud, Slocum thought, this thing was not yet over.

He considered following Agent, but then he decided against it. Agent had insisted that he could take care of the whole Smoot gang alone, and Agent was the only representative of the law in the area. He was in charge. So be it. Let him handle things his own way. Slocum's only concern was the safety and welfare of Sammy Golden, Bradley, Sally and the other ranchers. He laughed at himself. His only concern should be his own worthless hide, but then, in spite of his better judgment, he was always getting himself into these kinds of scrapes, always getting himself involved in someone else's troubles.

Sally came walking over to stand beside him, calling his mind back to things at hand.

Everyone's gone home," she said. "I reckon you and me could go on back over to my ranch. Or will you be moving on now the trouble's over with?"

"I don't think I'll be moving on just yet," he said.

Golden came walking toward them with Julie clinging to his arm. Both of the young people had broad smiles on their faces.

"Slocum, Sally," Golden said, "we got us something to tell you."

"The way you're grinning," said Slocum, "I might could guess it, but you go on and tell."

"Me and Julie," Golden said, "we're getting hitched."

"Congratulations," Slocum said, and he thought that this too was a premature announcement. Everyone was getting too all-fired excited too fast.

"I hope you'll both be very happy together," said Sally.

"I know we will," Julie said.

"Yeah. Me too," said Golden.

If you don't get your ass killed being careless, Slocum thought, but he kept that thought, like the others, to himself.

U.S. Marshal Dan "Road" Agent walked his horse through the gate of Sam Golden's ranch. Keeping his eyes peeled, he proceeded slowly to the front of the ranch house. Two men lounged on the front porch. As he approached, the two men stood up to face him. He stopped his horse just a few feet away.

"I'm looking for Smoot," he said.

The men eyeballed him suspiciously. The badge on Agent's vest was showing clearly.

"And who might you be?" said one of the men.

"I'm United States Marshal Dan Agent."

"Wait here," said one of the men. "I'll tell Mr. Smoot you're here."

He turned and went through the front door. The other man stayed on the porch staring at Agent. Agent's eyes flicked back and forth from the man to the door. In a moment, the other man returned followed by yet a third. The third man stepped forward.

"I'm Smoot," he said. "What do you want?"

"Smoot," said Agent, "you're under arrest. You and these other two and anyone else who might be on this place."

"What's the charge?"

"Land fraud and suspicion of murder."

"I have a land grant for this valley," Smoot said, "and in addition to that, I'm securing deeds to all the ranches. As for the murder charge, it's ridiculous. It's trumped up. I never killed anyone, and you can't prove that I did."

"That ain't for me to worry about," said Agent. "I just arrest them. The court does all the rest. You coming along peaceably?"

"Well, I—"

"I ain't," said one of the two hired men, and he reached for his six-gun. In a flash, Agent's right-hand Colt was out and roared, and the man clutched at his chest, staggered back to fall against the wall, then slid down to a sitting position. He was dead. The other man stopped still, his hand opened as if going for the gun.

"I quit," he said. "I ain't going for it."

"Then reach for the buckle and drop the belt," Agent said.

The man did as he was told. Smoot stood still. He was not wearing a gun.

"All right," Agent said, "the both of you start walking toward that corral. Catch up a couple of horses and saddle them. We're riding into town."

Inside the land office in Harleyville, Sim had finished the recording.

"You want to leave him like this?" Graves said.

"There's three of us and just one of him," said Tarance. "If it comes to it, it'd be his word against ours, and by then we'll have all them deeds signed to back up what he done here. He can't hurt us none."

Graves walked back over close to Sim and gave him a cold, hard stare.

"He better not even try," he said.

"Let's go," said Tarance.

They walked outside to their horses, and just then they saw Smoot and the other two men riding up to the hitch rail in front of the sheriff's office and jail. There was a fourth rider with them, a man in black.

"What's this?" Tarance said.

"Let's go see," said Graves.

They walked toward the jail diagonally across the street. Smoot and the others had dismounted and were slapping the reins of their horses around the rail.

"Let's go," Agent said.

"You're making a big mistake," said Smoot.

"Tell it to the judge," said Graves. "And it won't be one you bought or made up this time."

"Mr. Smoot," Tarance called out.

The men heading for the front door of the jailhouse stopped and turned. Agent stepped out in front.

"What's going on, Boss?"

"This man here says he's putting me in jail," Smoot said. "Something about land fraud and murder. I told him it's all a mistake."

Tarance and the other two with him had stopped in the middle of the street. Graves stepped a couple of steps out in front of the other two.

"I take it you don't want to go in that jail, Mr. Smoot," Graves said, pulling the black leather gloves tight on his hands.

"I'd rather not," said Smoot.

"You can leave it be, mister," said Agent, "or drop your guns and join him. It's your choice."

"I think there's another choice."

"It's still your choice."

"Not mine alone. You could turn around and walk inside that office and shut the door. We'll ride out of here and leave you alone."

"What's your name?" Agent said.

"Graves."

"The Gravedigger?"

"I get called that. Who are you?"

"United States Marshal Dan Agent."

"Road Agent?"

"I get called that too."

"There's folks that would make bets on what's about to happen here," Graves said.

"I expect so."

The men in the middle of the street moved away from Graves, and those up on the sidewalk in front of the jail moved away from Agent. Others in town stopped where they were and watched.

"Make your play, Road," Graves said.

"I told you," said Agent, "it's your choice."

None of the witnesses could say which man went for his gun first. It was as if it happened while everyone on the street blinked at once. Both guns were out and flashing and barking. Smoot fell to the sidewalk on his belly and covered his head with his hands. The other man Agent had arrested crouched in a doorway. Out in the street, Tarance and his cohort ran in opposite directions. A bullet from the marshal's gun ripped the hat off of Graves's head. Suddenly the shooting stopped. Both men were still standing, but a smear of blood began spreading over the white shirt and black vest of Agent. He was standing straight, his Colt held out in front of him, still pointed generally in the direction of the Gravedigger. His fingers relaxed and dropped the gun. His knees buckled, and he pitched forward, falling off the sidewalk and into the dirt street. United States Marshal Dan "Road" Agent was dead.

14

"Tarance," said Smoot, "mount up and get going right now while no one's watching you. Get out and get me those extra men. Now."

"It'll take me a few days," Tarance said.

"Then stop wasting time."

Tarance ran to where his horse waited, mounted up and headed out of town fast. He thought that his boss was probably right. He might have a chance this time. Since the ranchers had brought in the marshal, and the marshal had arrested Smoot, the ranchers had most likely relaxed. They wouldn't be watching to see if anyone was riding out to recruit new gunfighters.

Smoot watched Tarance for a moment, then turned to face Graves.

"That was damn good shooting," he said. "How did things go in the land office?"

"Everything's been taken care of," said the Gravedigger. "What now?"

"Let's get back out to the ranch," Smoot said. "I want to send some of the boys out to start collecting the deeds to back up what you just got done here in the land office."

"You want me to ride with them?"

"I want you to stick close to me," Smoot said. "Let's go."

*　　*　　*

Elisha Johnson, one of the small ranchers of Whistling Valley, watched through the front window of the general store. When Smoot and his bunch had ridden out of sight, Johnson went outside and mounted his own horse. He headed for the Ringy Dingy.

"Reckon how Agent's doing with Smoot?" Dave Bradley asked.

He was seated at the table in the Ringy Dingy ranch house, along with Golden, old Bradley and Slocum. They were drinking coffee. Sally and Julie were both in the kitchen preparing the noon meal.

"I 'magine we'll hear something before long now," old Bradley said.

There was a knock on the front door, and all heads turned in that direction. The door opened slightly, and Lefty stuck in his head.

"Mr. Bradley?"

"Come on in, Lefty," Bradley said. "Sit down and have a cup of coffee with us."

"Thank you," Lefty said, walking to the table and taking a seat.

Bradley called into the kitchen, and a moment later Sally brought out a cup for Lefty.

"What's up?" Dave asked.

"Just thought you'd like to know," said Lefty. "I was out to the road while ago, and I seen that Marshal Agent ride outa the—well—outa Sam Golden's place there—and he had Smoot and one other feller in tow."

"You mean he arrested them and was taking them in?" Dave asked.

"That's sure what it looked like," Lefty said.

"Well, that's that then," Dave said. "Sam, you can ride over and move into your ranch house any time you take a notion."

Golden gave out a little nervous laugh. "I don't know," he said. "It sounds too easy to me—after all we've been through."

"What all we've been through," Dave argued, "has been on account of Smoot, so with Smoot under arrest, it's all over with. What could be more simpler than that?"

"Well," Golden said, "maybe you're right."

Slocum listened to all this talk but kept quiet. His opinions, he thought, were best kept in his own head.

It was after dinner when Elisha Johnson rode up to the ranch house. Slocum and Bradley were sitting on the front porch smoking cigars. They stood up to greet Johnson as he stopped his horse. He was obviously agitated over something, and he had ridden up in a hurry.

"Elisha," Bradley asked "what is it?"

"I just come from town," Johnson said, not bothering to dismount. "I was in the general store, and I happened to look out the window. I seen that marshal riding in with Smoot and one of his gun hands."

"Lefty said that Agent had arrested Smoot and one other man," Bradley said.

"Yeah, well, he arrested them all right," said Johnson, "but then that Tarance and another man come out of the land office. They seen what was going on, and they walked over toward the jail. They stopped in the middle of the street. I couldn't hear what they was saying, but the stranger, he talked to the marshal. Then they both went to shooting. I couldn't make out who shot first, they was both so fast. But when it was all over, the marshal fell dead. Smoot and the others, they rode outa town big as you please."

"Damn," said Bradley.

"I was afraid of something like that," Slocum said. "This stranger—what did he look like?"

"Slender feller. Dressed all in black. Had a mustache. Wore two guns. Low."

"The Gravedigger's here," Slocum said.

"The Gravedigger," Bradley repeated.

"We knew he'd been sent for," Slocum said. "He got here fast."

"It was some sight," Johnson said. "Them two facing each other. Both dressed in black like that. Both of them faster'n a rattlesnake."

"Yeah," said Slocum. "There's not a hell of a lot of difference. Just the badge."

"And now one of them's dead," Bradley said, "and the one that's still living is on the wrong side."

Johnson decided to climb down off his horse. He did so slowly, and then he took a couple of steps toward Bradley and Slocum.

"Well, what do we do now?" he asked.

"There ain't nothing to be done but out and out war," Bradley said. "We'll get some men together and attack their headquarters."

"That won't hardly do," Slocum said.

"Why not?"

"In the first place," Slocum said, "we'd have to be sure that they were all there in one place—all together. Smoot, Graves, all of them. In the second place, if they have good cover, like if they're in the ranch house, Graves can take on six or more men just by himself."

"Oh, now, surely—"

"I mean it," Slocum said, interrupting old Bradley. "Remember Agent telling us those tales of how he took on whole gangs single-handed and won? Well, he was a blowhard, that's true, but those tales he told us were true. And Graves took Agent, didn't he? I've seen Graves in action. I was on the same side of a range war with him one time. He's deadly, and he's worth any five or six men I've ever seen. But on top of that, he's as cold-blooded and deadly as any snake. I'd hate to have to face him head on."

"Well, what then?"

"Someone needs to get word back to the governor what happened here," said Slocum. "That's the first thing. And then we ought to find out what Tarance and Graves were doing in the land office."

"Say," Bradley said, "that's right." He turned on Johnson again. "You did say they come out of the land office, didn't you?"

"That's right."

"They're up to something," Slocum said. "They haven't given up yet."

*   *   *

Johnson headed home, and Slocum and Bradley headed into town. They still had time to get into Harleyville before the land office and the telegraph office would close for the day. Johnson had a longer ride ahead of him. His small ranch was on the far reaches of the valley, and he would just make it back before darkness set in.

In Harleyville, Bradley and Slocum split up. Slocum went to the telegraph office. Inside, he wrote out a note. He handed it to the man behind the counter.

"Send this to the governor's office," he said.

The clerk read the note and looked up at Slocum with something like terror written across his face.

"Go on," Slocum said.

The little, timid clerk began tapping out the message. "Agent killed by Graves," it said. "Graves hired by Smoot. Please advise. War is coming here."

When the clerk finished his tapping, Slocum paid him.

"You send that just like I wrote it?" he asked.

"Yes, sir."

"How soon will we get an answer?"

"This late in the day," the clerk said, "it won't be before sometime tomorrow morning. Maybe tomorrow afternoon. It's hard to say. Wait a minute. This is Friday. Might not be anyone in the office to receive the message till Monday."

"All right," Slocum said. He turned and walked out of the office, and he saw Bradley on the sidewalk walking toward him. They met about halfway between the two offices.

"You get the message sent off?" Bradley asked.

"Yeah, but we might not get an answer till Monday. That's what the man said."

"I was afraid of that," said Bradley.

"So what did you find out?"

"Tarance and Graves and one other Smoot man went into the land office," said Bradley, "and they forced the clerk to record all the deeds to the whole valley in the name of Smoot."

"That won't hold up in court, will it?"

"Not unless Smoot can get his hands on all the deeds and have them signed over to him," Bradley said. "He's putting the cart before the horse. If it was done legal, he'd get the deed signed over to him, and then he'd take it in to the office to have it recorded."

"Then he must be planning to get the horse and bring it along behind," Slocum said. "And with Graves backing his play, he just might be able to do it. I'm afraid you sent all the ranchers home early."

"Yeah," Bradley said. "It's looking that way, ain't it?"

Elisha Johnson rode slowly. It had been a long ride for his old horse, and he was being kind to it, as well as to himself. The sun was low in the western sky as he turned into his gate. There was no need for him to guide the old horse, it made straight for the corral. Johnson let it have its head. At the corral, he dismounted, opened the gate, and led the horse in. He unsaddled it and turned it loose. Then he headed slowly for his house. In the darkness, he did not see the two horses standing on the far side of the house.

Inside the house, he found a lantern and struck a match to light it. As he looked up from the lantern, he saw in its light two ugly faces grinning at him. He did not know the names of the two men, but he recognized them as Smoot hands. His heart skipped a couple of beats, and his voice caught in his throat. He looked from one face to the other with nervous eyes.

"Evening, Mr. Johnson," said the face with a gap in its front teeth.

"What—what do you want with me?" Johnson stammered.

"Mr. Smoot sent us over to get the deed to this place," Gap-tooth said. "You agreed to sell it to him."

"I never agreed to sell."

"That ain't the way we heard it," Gap-tooth said. "You ain't trying to back out on the deal are you? Mr. Smoot wouldn't like that. Why don't you just make this quick and easy and get that deed out and sign it and hand it over to us?"

"I—I don't want to sell," Johnson said.

"We can do this easy or we can do it rough," said Gap-tooth.

"Why don't you just get out of my house and leave me alone?"

"You afraid you won't get paid? You'll get paid all right. Just get the deed and sign it, and we'll be on our way."

Johnson began shaking his head nervously. "No," he said. "No. I won't."

The silent one stood up and stalked slowly over to Johnson, who backed away in fright. When he had backed into the wall and could go no farther, the silent one grabbed a handful of Johnson's hair and jerked his head back, slapping him across the face several times with his other hand.

"You going to find that deed for us?" Gap-tooth asked.

"No," said Johnson. "Get out."

The silent one drove a fist into his stomach that doubled Johnson over. Then he drove a fist into the side of Johnson's head, knocking him to the floor. His big boot kicked Johnson in the ribs, again and again. Then it kicked his head.

"Hey," Gap-tooth said, "don't kill him."

The silent one reached down and took hold of the front of Johnson's shirt, dragging Johnson to his feet. Then he swung him around and dropped him into a chair. Johnson slumped there half conscious. Blood ran down the side of his head and onto his shirt.

"Mr. Johnson," said Gap-tooth, "I told you we could make this easy. You want us to get out of here and leave you alone, just get out that deed and sign it. We'll get right outa here, and we'll even give you till tomorrow night to move out. What do you say?"

Johnson sat breathing heavily. The silent one raised his hammy fist.

"All right," said Johnson. "All right. I'll do it."

He tried to stand, but he was unable to do so.

"Just tell me where it's at," Gap-tooth said.

Johnson pointed across the room to a small secretary. Gap-tooth went over to it and pulled open a drawer. He pulled out some papers, eliminating some and tossing them aside. Then he held one up and looked at it closely. He grinned and walked to the table, opening out the deed and smoothing it on the table. He found a pen and a bottle of ink on the secretary and brought them to the table. Dipping the pen in the bottle, he held it in front of Johnson. Johnson did not move. The silent one took a handful of hair and twisted Johnson's head to one side.

"No, no," Johnson said. "Wait."

He reached for the pen. Laboriously, he leaned forward and wrote his name on the deed. Gap-tooth took it up and looked at it. Smiling, he folded it and tucked it inside his shirt.

"Thank you, Mr. Johnson," he said. "It's been a pleasure doing business with you."

He walked to the door, opened it and walked out into the night. The silent one did not follow him immediately. Instead, he smashed his fist into the side of Johnson's head once more, knocking him to the floor again. Then he kicked the helpless Johnson again over and over. He kicked the ribs and the head. At last, the toes of his boots bloody, he stopped and went outside. Gap-tooth was waiting in front of the house with both horses.

"Are we ready to go?" he asked.

The other one nodded.

"And Mr. Johnson is—"

The silent one answered only with a cold, hard stare. The two mounted up and rode away.

It was almost noon the following day when Elisha Johnson, battered and bloody, sagging in his saddle, rode slowly up to the porch of the Ringy Dingy ranch house. No one was out on the porch. He thought about yelling out for help, but he did not have the strength. He sat there, slipping slowly but surely to one side. He tried to sit straight and keep his seat. He thought about dismounting deliberately, but he lacked even enough strength to do that. He hoped someone would step out of the house or come along from elsewhere to find him there before he fell off the horse, for he knew that was coming.

Dave Bradley had just come back from riding herd. He rode into the corral and turned loose his horse. He knew that the noon meal would be on the table soon, and he was hungry. He started walking toward the house, and he saw that someone was there on horseback, just sitting there. He walked closer, and he could see that there was something wrong with the man. He began to trot. Closer yet, he recognized Elisha Johnson, and he saw the blood, and then he saw Johnson slowly slip from his saddle. He ran hard, and he managed to catch Johnson just in time to ease his landing on the ground.

"Elisha?" he said, holding Johnson's head up. "Elisha?"

Johnson rolled his eyes just a little.

Dave looked anxiously toward the house.

"Hey, Dad," he yelled. "Sammy. Someone. Help. Help me out here."

The door opened on the porch, and Sally stepped out. She stopped and stared. Then she rushed down the steps and hurried over to Dave's side.

"It's Elisha Johnson," she said. "What happened?"

"Damned if I know," Dave said. "I just found him here like this. We got to get him inside."

Sam Golden came out of the house then.

"Sammy," Sally said. "Come quick and give us a hand."

The three of them managed to get Johnson into the house and into a bedroom where they laid him out on the bed. Soon old Bradley, Slocum and Julie were also there. Sally took charge, ordering hot water and clean rags. She had Bradley and Golden strip Johnson's clothes off, so his wounds could all be located and dressed. While she was working on him, old Bradley spoke up.

"Elisha," he said. "Elisha, can you hear me?"

Johnson moaned.

"Elisha, who done this to you?"

"Smoot," Johnson said, his voice barely audible. "Smoot. He got my deed."

15

The next morning, several ranchers came in to the Ringy Dingy. Two of them told Bradley they had been visited by the bullies from Smoot, and they had both signed over their deeds. One of them had been beaten, but not nearly so badly as had Johnson. He had given up quicker. The other had been scared into signing without any violence. The fear of it was enough in his case. Both ranchers said that Smoot's men had given them twenty-four hours to clear out. A few others came by because they had heard about the killing of Agent or they had heard about the bullying and beating of Johnson and the others. Pretty soon a full meeting was in progress.

"Slocum wired the governor on Friday," Bradley told them. "It was late in the day, so we won't likely hear nothing till Monday. My suggestion is that we gather everyone up back here again and wait till we get an answer. If we're all together here, like we was before, they can't get to us."

"That depends," said one of the ranchers.

"What's it depend on?" Bradley asked.

"I heard that right after that gravediggin' feller killed the marshal, that Tarance rode outa town," the man said. "He wasn't headed back for the ranch. He was headed out the other direction."

"Damn," said Dave Bradley. "He's gone out to hire on more guns, and we weren't watching for it this time."

"So depending on how fast he gets back and how many he's

129

got," the other man said, "we could be in for some real trouble."

"All the more reason to get ever'one back together," Bradley said. "Let's get some riders out to warn them and round them up."

For the rest of that day, some of the ranchers and several of Bradley's hands rode throughout the valley. They went to each ranch and told the owners what had happened. The ranchers all agreed to return to the Ringy Dingy once again. At two ranches they found people who had already been visited by the two Smoot men and had signed over their deeds. Those men went along with the others anyway. Slocum had gone out with Dave Bradley. They were approaching the last ranch on their list. As they drew near the ranch house, Slocum saw that two saddled horses waited outside.

"What do you make of that?" he asked.

"He's got visitors," said Dave.

"Let's move on up kind of easy," said Slocum.

They walked the horses up to the house and dismounted. Slocum made a motion for Dave to stay put, and then he walked around the corner keeping close to the wall. He sidled up to a window there and peered in cautiously. He saw the rancher in a chair being menaced by two men. He knew it was the two that Smoot had sent out to collect the deeds. Carefully, he made his way back to the front of the house, and again he motioned for Dave to keep quiet. He pointed to the house and to the two saddled horses. Dave understood. Slocum and Dave both drew out their six-guns and cocked them. Then Slocum stepped up close to the front door. He shoved it open suddenly and stepped quickly inside. Dave followed hard on his heels.

The two Smoot men whirled, surprised. One man reached for his gun, and Slocum shot him through the chest. He fell back across the table. The other man stuck his hands in the air quickly.

"Don't shoot," he said. "Don't shoot."

"Maybe we shouldn't shoot him, Slocum," said Dave. "Maybe we ought to take him back to the ranch and hang him."

"No," the man said, "now wait a minute. We was just doing our job is all."

"Shut up," Dave said. He looked toward the rancher whose face showed much relief. "You all right, Mr. Fraser?"

"Thanks to you two," Fraser said. "These men were threatening me if I didn't get out my deed and sign it over to Smoot."

"We know," Slocum said. "They've already collected several of them."

They told Fraser why they had been riding over the valley, and he agreed to ride back with them to the Ringy Dingy. He first got out his deed and took it with him for safekeeping. Slocum and Dave took the Smoot man's gun away from him and tied his hands behind his back. They hauled the body out of Fraser's house and tossed it across the dead man's saddle. Then they shoved the live one up into his saddle and headed for the Ringy Dingy.

Most of the ranchers were already there by the time Slocum and Dave arrived back at the Bradley ranch house with Fraser, their prisoner and their other baggage. The ones who had given up their deeds identified the two men as the ones who had harassed them. The live one, his hands still tied securely behind his back, was taken into the bedroom where Johnson lay. Johnson had recovered some from his ordeal.

"You recognize this man, Johnson?" Bradley asked.

"It's the one that stomped me," Johnson said.

"Get him out of here," said Bradley, and Dave and Slocum dragged the man back outside. On the porch, Dave gave the man a hard shove, and he fell headlong down the stairs sprawling at the feet of a small mob of angry ranchers.

"He's the one that stomped up Johnson," Dave said.

Two ranchers reached down and pulled the man to his feet. The rest pushed and shoved at one another in an attempt to get at the man. They screamed and shouted. They punched his face, his ribs, his gut. They pulled his hair out in clumps. In no time at all, the man's face was a bloody mess. He had several cracked ribs, a broken nose and a broken jaw. For a while, they held him up on his feet, but at last they let him fall to the ground. Then several of the ranchers crowded around him, kicking and stomping.

On the porch, Dave, old Bradley, Slocum and Golden were watching.

"They're going to kill him," Golden said.

"Let them," said Dave. "You seen what he did to Johnson."

"Stop them, Dave," Slocum said. "We got a use for him."

Dave looked at his father. Old Bradley said, "Do as he says."

With some difficulty, Dave managed to stop the beating. The wretched victim of the mob lay writhing and whimpering in the dirt, battered and bloody, his hands still tied.

"Put him on his horse," Slocum said. "Tie the two horses together and send them home."

"We going to send a message with them?" Dave asked.

"They are the message," Slocum said.

Holland was on the porch of the Smoot headquarters when the two horses came walking slowly toward the corral. He stood up and stared wide-eyed. Then he turned back and jerked open the door.

"Hey, Boss," he yelled, "you better come and see this."

In a moment, Smoot was on the porch beside Holland. The two horses were making their way toward the corral.

"Stop them," Smoot said.

Holland ran out and stopped the horses, and the badly beaten man fell sideways out of his saddle.

"Who is it?" Smoot called out.

Holland bent over to look at the one on the ground. "It's Pudge," he called out. He straightened up and walked to the far side of the other horse. Taking the dangling head by its hair, he lifted it for a look. "This one here is Art. He's dead."

"Well, get Pudge into the bunkhouse," Smoot said. "Get him in bed."

While Holland saw to that chore, Smoot went back in the house. A moment later he reemerged with Graves walking alongside him. They walked to the bunkhouse and found Holland hovering over the badly battered Pudge. At the bedside, Smoot said, "Pudge. What happened? Who done this?"

Pudge moaned.

"Tell us what happened," Smoot demanded.

Pudge sucked in a breath and seemed to try to make some sounds.

"Hell, Boss," Holland said, "he's damn near dead."

Graves shoved his way between Smoot and Holland and took Pudge by the shirt front, lifting him off the bed. Pudge cried out in pain. Graves looked him straight in the eyes.

"Who did it?" he asked.

"Ranchers," Pudge managed. "Ringy Dingy."

Graves dropped him back to the bed and stepped back.

"That what you wanted to know?" he asked.

"Yeah," Smoot said. He looked at the bloody Pudge with disgust. "Now what the hell am I going to do about him?"

The Gravedigger slipped out his right-hand six-gun and cocked it in one smooth motion. He aimed it at Pudge's chest. Pudge's eyes were almost swollen shut. Even so, they opened wide in fear.

"No," he said in a weak but frightened voice. "No."

The Gravedigger pulled the trigger, and what to do with Pudge was no longer a problem for Smoot. Graves ejected the spent shell and put in a new bullet. Then he slipped the deadly weapon back into the holster. Smoot shot a glance at Holland.

"Get rid of him," he said. "And Art too. Then put away the horses. When you're done, get back to the porch."

He turned to leave the bunkhouse, followed by P. T. Graves.

"Sure, Boss," Holland said. He watched as the other two left the room. Then he looked at the mess on the bed that had been Pudge. He was almost sickened by the sight. He did not really want to touch that mess, nor the one outside. But he had just seen the Gravedigger in cold-blooded action, and he was afraid not to do what he had been told to do. He wished at that moment that he had never met Smoot, and he wondered if he could possibly manage to sneak away in the night without being stopped. He wondered if he would have the guts to try.

On the porch of the ranch house, Smoot stopped.

"We'd better stay here," he said, "till Holland gets back. I don't want to take a chance on someone riding in here and surprising us."

"They got to you, did they?" Graves said.

"What do you mean?"

"When someone beats someone nearly to death like that, and then stops short, there's a reason. He was sent back here along with the dead one to warn us. Mostly to scare us. That's all. Don't let it get to you."

He turned and walked into the house, leaving Smoot alone on the porch. Smoot did not move. If those bastards over at the Ringy Dingy had done that to frighten him, well, they had succeeded. He felt a certain amount of security with the presence of the Gravedigger, but even the Gravedigger couldn't handle a whole army of angry ranchers, not alone. Smoot longed for the return of Tarance with at least a dozen fighting men.

And then he had a sudden new worry. It wouldn't matter until the ranchers were all defeated and out of the way, but when that time did come, it could be a major worry. The way Graves was behaving, Smoot thought, he just might try to take everything over for himself. And who would be able to stop him? He thought about telling Tarance when he returned to wait until they knew that they had won, and then to shoot the gunfighter in the back without warning. Yes. He would give Tarance that instruction just as soon as he possibly could.

The Gravedigger was just inside the house. He had poured himself a cup of coffee and sat down to relax. He was getting a little impatient for some real action. He liked his work, and he abhorred being idle for too long at a time. Of course, he knew that Smoot was right about one thing. Even P. T. Graves could not take on the whole valley alone. Once Tarance returned with reinforcements, they would be able to fight it out with all the ranchers, if need be. Then he would get plenty of action, and then he would be able to single out that Slocum, the gunfighter for the ranchers. Graves remembered Slocum from a previous range war. He recalled that they had been on the same side that time. It didn't matter. Graves always fought for the side that paid the most.

He remembered Slocum, all right, and he knew that Slocum was good. There were not too many gunslingers out there that

Slocum couldn't take easily. There were not too many, but
P. T. Graves was one. He had seen Slocum in action, and he
knew that he could take Slocum. He thought that he could drill
him even before Slocum cleared leather. He was anxious to
find out if that would be the case. And Slocum was pretty well
known. His would be a good notch to have on his six-gun's
handle. He wondered if he would take Slocum with his right
hand or his left. He didn't think it would matter much. One
hand was about as fast as the other. Either way, Slocum would
die.

He thought about the beaten man, the man he had just shot
and put out of his misery. He didn't think that was the work
of Slocum. He didn't remember Slocum to be that kind. But
it occurred to him that maybe Slocum had stopped the beating.
Maybe those ranchers would have beat Pudge to death had not
Slocum stepped in. At that point, it would be like Slocum to
send the man and the other dead one back as a warning. Oh,
yes, he was looking forward to his meeting with Slocum.

And once that was done, the job here would be over. He
considered Smoot. The man had gone to a great deal of trouble
and incredible risk to acquire control over this Whistling
Valley, and Graves wondered why. Personally, he did not believe the ranches to be worth the risk and the expense. And
he knew that Smoot was no rancher. Why then did he want
all those ranches? He would have to find out the reason one
way or another, and if he was right, if there was some un-
known reason for going after all that land, it would be worth
a great deal of money, and the man who controlled the valley
would be king of the valley and of nearby Harleyville.

Smoot was not tough. Graves could tell that Smoot was
afraid of him. When the time was right, Graves thought, he
would take over the whole operation from Smoot. He would
be king of the valley. It would be a foolish thing indeed to
win the prize for someone else, and he was certain that Smoot
could not win it without him. Graves would be the kingmaker.
Why not go one more step and be king?

On Monday morning, Slocum saddled his big Appaloosa and
rode into Harleyville early. He went straight to the telegraph

office and learned that there was as yet no response from the governor. He rode over to a nearby hash house and ordered himself a breakfast. Following the breakfast, he sat there for two more cups of coffee. Finally, he went back to the office, and the clerk handed him a note.

"It just came through," he said.

Slocum took the paper and looked at it.

"Thanks," he said. He pocketed the note, went back outside, mounted up and rode back to the ranch. He had encountered no Smoot men all the way. That convinced him all the more that Smoot was shorthanded. He didn't have much except for the Gravedigger. Of course, the Gravedigger was a hell of a lot to have. Back on the Ringy Dingy, Slocum went inside the ranch house to find Bradley.

"Here it is," he said, handing the note to Bradley.

Bradley read it quickly. Then he read it again.

"Well," he said, "I guess it's good news and bad news."

"Yeah," Slocum agreed.

Dave walked in just then.

"What is it?" he asked.

"The governor's response," old Bradley said. "He'll be sending us some deputy marshals—at least four, he says, but they won't be able to start from there for another four days."

"A lot can happen in four days," Dave said.

"That's the bad part," said Slocum.

"So what do we do?"

"We're all here together," Bradley said. "We wait and watch. The governor wants us to try to hold out and let the law handle it. We'll try. But we'll stay ready. If Smoot makes the first move, we'll fight him to the end. But as long as he sits tight, we'll sit tight."

"One more thing," Slocum said.

"Yeah?"

"When those four deputies show up," said Slocum, "we don't let them ride over there after Smoot by themselves. Not with the Gravedigger there."

Smoot heard a commotion out in the yard, and he ran for the door, calling out to Graves at the same time.

"Someone's coming," he said. "A bunch of them."

He waited at the door for Graves to step up beside him. Then he pulled open the door and peered out timidly. He could see the riders out there in the dark.

"Who's there?" he called out.

"Just me, Boss."

Smoot heaved a tremendous sigh of relief when he recognized the voice of Tarance. He went out on the porch and Graves followed him. Smoot's eyes slowly adjusted to the darkness outside, and he looked at Tarance sitting on his horse smiling. Behind him on both sides were other riders. Smoot tried to count them.

"Tarance, welcome back," he said, and he sure did mean it too. "How many you got there?"

"A baker's dozen," Tarance said. "Thirteen men. All good men."

"Climb down and welcome, boys," Smoot said. "Come on inside for a drink."

Graves watched as the new men stepped up onto the porch to go inside the house. Some of the faces were new to him. Some he recognized. It looked to him as if Tarance had done a pretty good job all right. It would just make his own job that much easier. As good as he was, he was no fool. He knew that he couldn't fight that whole bunch of valley ranchers all by himself. The only thing was that he wanted Slocum for himself. He would have to make sure that all these men knew that. Don't touch Slocum. Leave Slocum for himself.

16

There were a couple of lookouts on duty down by the road and a couple of men riding herd, but mostly all the ranchers and all of Bradley's ranch hands were sitting down for their big noon meal. Bradley himself, Dave, Golden, Slocum, Sally and Julie were eating in the ranch house. The others were out at the bunkhouse. Bradley was wondering how his food stores would hold up if this Smoot business wasn't resolved soon.

"Reckon how soon that damned Tarance will get back with some new gun hands?" Dave said.

"Dave," said Bradley, admonishing, "we don't talk about that at the table. It ain't good for the digestion."

Just then a couple of shots sounded out in the yard. Slocum jumped up quick and headed for the door. The rest were not far behind him. Out on the porch, Slocum saw Lefty on horseback, his six-gun in his hand. Bradley stepped out the door.

"What the hell is up?" Bradley demanded.

About a dozen men coming our way," Lefty called out. "Tarance is riding in front of them."

"There's the answer to your question," Slocum said to Dave.

"This ain't so good for the digestion either," Dave said.

"Get your guns," Bradley yelled. "Someone get over to the bunkhouse and tell everyone there."

"I'll do it," said Lefty, and he spurred his horse, turning it in that direction.

*   *   *

Out on the road, Tarance turned into the Ringy Dingy gate.
As he did, he pulled out his six-gun and yelled over his shoulder.

"Get ready, men, and shoot anything that moves."

The outlaw gang, brandishing weapons, began to whoop and
holler. Some even fired preliminary shots into the air. They
were about halfway to the ranch house when they were met
by a band of ranchers and cowhands. Two of the new gunslingers fell at the first volley. Tarance turned his horse and
rode to the rear of his gang. Men on both sides dismounted,
searching for whatever cover they could find.

A rancher fell dead. Lefty took a bullet in his left shoulder,
but he kept firing back. Dave Bradley got himself one of the
outlaws, and so did Sam Golden. The range war was on, hot
and heavy. The air was filled with gunsmoke and the stink of
burnt powder. Ears were ringing on both sides from the blasts
of the bullets. Two outlaw horses were wounded. So were two
outlaws.

"Let's get outa here," Tarance cried out.

The outlaws who could manage it, climbed back onto their
horses and headed for the road. Dave Bradley shot one in the
back as he fled. With the able-bodied outlaws well down the
lane toward the gate, Bradley's men began walking forward.
They disarmed the wounded outlaws and examined the dead
bodies. Slocum recognized one of the live ones and two of the
dead. He had worked with one of them once.

"I guess we by God showed them," said Dave.

"What do we do with these wounded ones?" Golden asked.

"Kill them," said Dave, and before anyone could say any
different, if anyone had a mind to, he jerked out his own revolver and shot the one nearest himself. Then he looked
around and shot the other one. Old Bradley opened his mouth
as if to speak, but he stopped himself. What the hell, he
thought. They'd have done the same to us.

"Someone'll have to bury the carcasses," he said.

"I'll see to it," said Dave. "Hey, Lefty."

Lefty walked over to his side.

"Yeah, Dave?"

"Lefty, see to it—hey. You're hurt."

"It ain't too bad," Lefty said.

"Well, get your ass back to the house. We'll get that took care of."

He called out to another of the hands and told him to grab a couple more men and dig some holes to throw the bodies in. Then he accompanied Lefty on his way back to the ranch house. As Bradley stepped up beside Slocum, he said, "Well, Slocum, what do you think?"

"It's damn sure started now," said Slocum.

"We give them a hell of a fight though, didn't we?"

"I didn't see Graves anywhere."

"No. I didn't either. Where the hell are those damn deputies anyway?"

Slocum didn't bother answering that question. He didn't think it was meant to be answered. He was wondering about something else anyhow. With all the lead that had been flying around, he had the distinct impression that no one had taken a shot at him. Not one.

Four men were busy digging graves, the guard was doubled, and in the house, Sally was busy patching up Lefty's shoulder. Slocum followed Bradley into the house. Julie offered coffee. What was left of the meal was cold, and she offered to heat it up, but no one was interested just then. Bradley and Slocum did accept the offer of coffee. They sat in the living room in easy chairs.

"What should we do now, Slocum?" Bradley asked.

"Nothing different, as I see it," Slocum answered. "Lefty saw them coming and gave us warning. We were able to drive them off. Their losses were greater than ours. If we tried to do anything different, we might not be so lucky."

"If that's what you say, then that's what we'll do. It's just that, I keep feeling like we oughta do something."

"We did plenty today. We just need to make sure we're ready for anything. That's all."

"Do you think they'll try the same thing again?"

"Maybe. Remember though, they picked off a man riding herd that one time. We need to make sure the men back that way are just as alert as the ones out front. They might try the same thing, or they might try something different. It's hard to say. Especially with that Gravedigger over there."

"But he didn't even come around today."

"A fight like this one, he wouldn't have made much difference. The other thing is that ole Smoot might've wanted to keep him close what with most everyone else away from the ranch."

"Like a personal bodyguard, huh?"

"Yeah. Bradley, I got something bothering me."

"What is it?"

"I got a real strong sense that no one out there today took a shot at me."

"Hell, ever'one was shooting ever'whichaway," Bradley said. "Ain't no way you could tell a thing like that."

"Did you feel like you were being shot at?"

"Well, yeah, but—"

"I sure didn't."

"What're you getting at, Slocum?"

"I don't know. I sure can't figure it out."

Dave came in the front door just then. He didn't slow down. He headed straight for the table and sat down where he had been before the fracas started. He took a bite. Then he hollered out, "Hey, Julie. You think you could heat this stuff up for me?"

Bradley looked at Slocum.

"I guess I raised that boy up tough," he said.

"You know what?" said Slocum. "I think I'll join him."

"We never made it to the ranch house," Tarance said. "They met us about halfway."

"They were ready for you," Graves said.

"So how did it go?" asked Smoot.

"Well, it was a hell of a fight. I can tell you that much."

"How many of them did you get?" Graves asked.

"It was hard to tell. Hell, there was bullets flying ever'where, men running around here and there, horses jumping and screaming. I can't say how many we hit."

"What about Slocum?" asked Graves. "Was he there?"

"Yeah. He was there. I seen him. He wasn't hit though."

"How many men did we lose?" asked Smoot.

"Five men killed and two wounded," said Tarance. "Two horses wounded."

"How bad wounded?" said Smoot.

"I don't know. We just left them behind."

"The men?"

"Oh. No. The horses. Well, uh, one man has got a hole in his left thigh, or was it the right? The other'n has a busted shoulder. They ain't hurt bad, but they ain't gonna be good for much for a while."

"So you brought me twelve new man," said Smoot, "and today you lost seven."

"It sounds to me like you lost the fight," said Graves.

"Well, hell," Tarance said, "we got the damn war started."

"It's nothing to start a war," said Graves. "Finishing one is what counts."

"Well, if you—" Tarance caught himself. He remembered just who he was talking to.

"If I what?" asked the Gravedigger.

"Well," Tarance said, looking at the floor and shuffling his feet, "if you got any suggestions for me, I'd be glad to hear them."

"First off," Graves said, "don't try that same stunt again. It's obvious they're watching for you. Put some men out, just a few, and if any of those ranchers venture out alone, try to get into town or anything like that, kill them."

"Okay," Tarance said. "I'll do it."

"Anyone except Slocum."

"Yeah. I understand. Anything else?"

"Just put out some watches. They might come back at us the way you went at them. If they do, we want to be able to turn the tables on them. Other than that, let's wait and see what they do."

"Well, that's all," Smoot said. "Go on. Get after it." He watched Tarance leave the room, and he was thinking about the way in which Graves had taken over. He was issuing orders as if he were the boss and not Smoot. Smoot didn't like it, but he didn't know what he could do about it. He had not yet had a chance to speak to Tarance alone. He knew, though, that he did not want to win this fight only to have the Grave-digger take it all away from him.

All the way over to the bunkhouse, Tarance muttered to him-self. He knew, of course, that the famous Gravedigger was a hell of a man to have on one's side in a fight, but he resented the man upbraiding him the way he had done. Tarance figured that Smoot was his boss. Graves seemed to be taking over, and Smoot just sat there and let him do it. He thought about quitting, but he had second thoughts right away. He knew Smoot's whole scheme, knew that it was a fraud right from the beginning. Smoot wouldn't just let him ride away with all that knowledge in his head. And Smoot had the Gravedigger to take care of any little chores like that.

He wondered, though, if Smoot was turning things over to Graves voluntarily or if Smoot, too, was afraid of the man. He decided that he would try to have a little talk with Smoot, see if he could figure out just where Smoot was at on this deal. In the meantime, he knew that he had better go right ahead and take care of those things the Gravedigger had told him to do. He sure wasn't ready for any kind of confrontation with the cold-blooded bastard.

"Your man Tarance is incompetent," Graves said to Smoot. "He needs to be replaced."

"Well," Smoot said, "I figured when you got here, you'd be in charge."

"As the general, yes, but I need a colonel in the field. One of the men Tarance brought back is a man named Smiley Slick. I know Smiley. I've known him for years. Worked with him a time or two. He'd be the choice."

"All right," Smoot said. He's taking over, he thought. He's making his move.

"Why don't you have the two of them brought in here for a talk?"

Smoot got up from his chair.

"I'll fetch them in," he said.

He left the house and headed for the bunkhouse where he

called Tarance out. Then he walked Tarance away from the bunkhouse a distance in the darkness. Looking over his shoulder, he spoke low.

"Tarance," he said, "Graves is making a move to take over."

"I kinda had that feeling myself," Tarance said.

"Just now he told me to replace you with a man named Slick."

"Smiley," said Tarance.

"It ain't my idea," said Smoot, "but I don't know what to do but go along with it for right now. I sure ain't gonna stand up to the Gravedigger."

"Yeah. I know what you mean."

"But listen here, Tarance. The first chance you get, where it's safe, you know, put a bullet in the man's back. We got to get rid of him any way we can."

Tarance felt a chill run down his spine.

"I'll keep my eyes open," he said.

"Right now you'd better go back in there and fetch out that Slick. Graves wants to see all of us at the ranch house."

"Me too?"

"You too."

After formally announcing the change, Graves told the others that he had a plan.

"You say all the ranchers are holed up at Bradley's place?"

"That's right," Tarance said.

"Then all the ranches in the whole damn valley except Bradley's are abandoned."

"Yeah. For now."

"And unguarded?"

"Yeah."

"Here's what you do," Graves said. "Take a few men and go around the valley. Set fire to some of them ranch houses. When the ranchers find out their property is in danger, they'll break up and head back for home to protect their own property. When they do that, you can pick them off easy."

"Yeah," Tarance said. "That oughta work."

"Damn right it'll work," Graves said. "Smiley, you take charge. Pick the men and pick the ranches. Pick some that are kinda close though. We want to make sure that they know what's going on."

"Okay, P. T.," Slick said. "We'll get right on it."

Sam Golden was standing guard near the gate when he saw the riders go by in the dark. He let them go for a while before he headed back to the ranch house. He found Slocum sitting on the porch puffing a cigar.

"Slocum. I just seen three men ride by. I think one of them was Tarance. Couldn't tell about the other two."

"Not headed for here?"

"They rode right past."

"All right, Sammy," Slocum said. "Go on back and keep watching. I'll find out what they're up to."

As Golden headed back for his post, Slocum ran out to the corral and saddled his Appaloosa. He rode fast to the gate and for a short distance down the road. Then he slowed. He did not want to warn the riders of his approach. He had walked the Appaloosa for a few miles when he topped a rise and saw the three men ahead and below. He watched as they turned down a lane leading to a small ranch house. He followed, keeping a safe distance. He was at the gate, and the men ahead had just reached the ranch house. Slocum moved ahead cautiously.

About half the distance to the house, he dismounted. He pulled the Colt out of his holster and walked ahead. Then he saw one of the men light a torch. He held it, waiting for the flame to take hold. They were planning to burn the house. He could not afford to move in closer. That would give them plenty of time to toss the torch. It was too far for a shot with the six-gun, but he had no choice. He snapped off a shot at the men. All three pulled guns and turned toward the shot. The torch was dropped to the ground where it burned harmlessly. Slocum took another shot. The outlaws ran for cover behind the far wall of the ranch house. They fired wild return shots at Slocum.

Behind the house, Slick stood still and quiet for a moment.

"There's only one man out there," he said. "Let's get to our horses and ride him down shooting."

They moved out quickly, mounted and headed for where they thought the man to be. They were almost on top of him before Tarance spotted him.

"There he is."

They all three started shooting at once, and bullets hit all around Slocum. He took quick aim and fired. One outlaw dropped dead. Slocum took another shot, too quick. It tore Slick's shirt sleeve.

"Come on," Slick yelled, turning his horse. He headed back for the road followed by Tarance. Slocum turned to fire after them, and as he did, he stepped into a hole and stumbled.

"Damn," he said. Straightening up, he saw that it would be senseless to chase the remaining two. He walked over to the burning torch, picked it up and snuffed it out. Then he started walking back to his horse. At least he had saved the house. And he had narrowed the outlaw ranks by one more. Damn. He wished it had been by three.

17

Back at the Ringy Dingy Ranch, Slocum spotted Golden and Julie sitting alone on the porch as he rode by. He rode on over to the corral, put away his Appaloosa and then walked back to the house.

"You two the only ones up yet?" he asked.

"Daddy's still up," said Julie. "He's in there in the living room."

"Everyone else has called it quits," Golden said. "I think. Except for the guards and the night riders, a course."

"Thanks."

Slocum went on in the house. He saw old man Bradley sitting alone in the living room in his favorite easy chair with a glass of whiskey on the table beside him. As Slocum came into the room Bradley looked up.

"Good evening," he said. "You're out kinda late."

"Howdy, Mr. Bradley," said Slocum. "I just followed three of those Smoot men over to a small ranch west of here. They were meaning to burn the house down. I stopped them, but two of them got away from me. I fell in a damn hole in the dark."

"But you stopped them from burning the house, and you got one of them," Bradley said.

"That's right."

"Kill him?"

"Yeah."

"Well, I guess we know then what they were planning to do next," Bradley said. "Here we are at a sort of standstill, and the ranchers are all huddled up here at my place again. The other ranches are all undefended, so Smoot has his bunch attacking the empty houses. Damn cowardly son of a bitch."

"I guess they figure that if the ranchers find out what they're up to, they'll go home to protect their property," Slocum said. "Then they can start in trying to pick them off one at a time again. If that doesn't work, when the ranchers discover they got no homes to go home to, maybe they'll clear out of here."

"Yeah. Something like that. You want a drink, Slocum?"

"I don't mind."

Slocum got himself a glass and poured it full of whiskey. Then he took a chair just across from old Bradley.

"Anything been happening around here while I was gone?"

"If it has been, it ain't come to my attention," Bradley said.

Slocum took himself a satisfying drink. "Mr. Bradley, you sure do stock good whiskey," he said.

"Life ain't worth living without good whiskey," the old man said. "Glad you like it."

"We still have men watching the road?"

"And the herd. You'd oughta finish that drink and get yourself some sleep. Try to relax a bit. No telling what might happen next."

"You're most likely right about that," Slocum said. He stood up with his drink in his hand and walked back to the front door. Opening the door, he looked out on the quiet, dark night. He noticed that Golden and Julie were no longer on the porch. He shut the door and went back to his chair and sat down again. He took another drink. "Trouble is," he said, "I don't feel sleepy. Say, what are you doing sitting up so late?"

"I don't feel none too sleepy my own self. Pour us another drink, Slocum."

Julie and Golden strolled along hand in hand. They had walked out beyond the corral, and they turned toward the barn. They walked slowly, enjoying one another's company. Now and then, one of them said something, but mostly they just walked along in silence. Sam Golden thought that he was the world's luckiest man. He had never known a girl, a woman, like Julie Bradley. He had seen good-looking women in saloons, of course, but Julie wasn't anything like them. She was young, beautiful, intelligent, and she was a ranch woman. She could cook, and she could ride a horse. She could even shoot if she had a reason. Golden couldn't imagine anything he would ever want in a woman that he did not already see in Julie.

And the best thing of all was that she seemed to want him as well. They had announced their intention of getting married as soon as possible, and, of course, if this mess with Smoot was all worked out satisfactorily, Golden would own his own ranch, and it would be adjacent to the Ringy Dingy, her own father's place. Sam Golden thought that he had fallen into a perfect situation. All it needed was to have Smoot cleaned out of it.

"Sam," Julie said. "Let's get married right away. Tomorrow."

"We can't ride out of here after a preacher," Golden said. "We're supposed to stay right here on the ranch."

"But I resent holding up our plans because of that man," she said. "He's running our lives for us."

"We'll be rid of him before long," Golden said. "The governor's sending us some deputies, you know."

"But we don't know how long it will take them to get here," she said, "and even when they do get here, we don't know how much good they'll do. Look what happened to Marshal Agent."

"I know," he said, "but that'll just make this bunch of deputies that much more cautious and that much more determined. Ain't nothing that a lawman hates like someone who's killed another lawman."

"I know," she said. "Let's just forget all that for now."

She pulled him in another direction. They continued walking along in silence. Golden wasn't worried about where she might be leading him. He was just content to be in her company. He, too, was anxious for the wedding day—and night—but he still wanted everything to be settled for her. He wanted to be worth something, to have his own property secure and have a home ready for her. He wanted the danger of range war to be behind them. He looked up and noticed that they were getting back close to the house, and he figured that she was ready to call it a day.

He veered toward the front porch, but she pulled him in another direction. He wondered what she was up to, but he didn't say anything. He just walked along with her. In a couple of minutes, they had come up close to the back wall of the house. Julie stopped beside a window. She looked at him and smiled. He looked at her, wondering what she was doing. She pulled his head down to kiss him full on the lips, and his whole body thrilled at the feel of it.

"The window's opened," she said.

Golden glanced at the window.

"Yeah," he said. "I can see that. Do you want it closed?"

"No," she said. "That's the window to my bedroom."

"Oh."

"Well?"

"Well—well, what, Julie?"

"Sam Golden," she said, "sometimes you're just too good. But I guess that's why I love you so much."

"I don't know what you're talking about," he said.

"All right then," she said. "We can't get off the ranch to go get a preacher and have our wedding. Right?"

"Yeah. That's right. For now. I wish—"

"Well, that Smoot can't run everything about our lives. So maybe we do have to wait for the wedding, but we don't have to wait for everything else."

"What do you mean, Julie?"

"Help me through that window," she said, "and then climb in after me, and I'll show you what I mean."

Even in the dark, Julie could see Golden's eyes open wide in astonishment.

"Do you mean—"

"Come on. Help me through."

Julie reached for the windowsill and started pulling, and Golden grabbed her by the waist to help. She scampered through to the inside.

"Come on," she whispered.

"I—I don't know."

Exasperated, she ripped at the front of her shirt to expose two lovely, round breasts with pert nipples, and she thrust them out the window at Golden. His eyes opened even wider than before, and his jaw dropped. Julie stuck a hand out toward him.

"Give me a hand," she said. He reached forward, and she took his hand and pressed its palm against a breast. Golden felt his knees weaken.

"Oh, my," he said.

"Do you know about that?" she said. "There's more. Are you coming in here after me or not?"

"I'm coming," he said. He grabbed the windowsill and clambered up, over and through to stand in front of her. She put her arms around his shoulders and pulled him close for another kiss. This one was wet and lingering. Golden felt a stirring in his loins.

"Julie," he said, "I love you, and I want you."

"I want you," she said, "and I want you right now."

She took the hat off his head and tossed it onto a chair nearby. Then she reached for the buckle of his gun belt. He grabbed the belt, and when she had the buckle undone, he laid the belt and gun aside. She was already unfastening the front of his shirt. With his shirt off and hers, she pressed herself against him once more, and he shuddered at the feel of her breasts against his bare chest. She backed off a little, took him by the hand and led him across the room. They sat side by side on the edge of the bed and pulled off their boots. Then she stood in front of him and unfastened her jeans. He stared. He was a little embarrassed, but he was more fascinated. He couldn't move his eyes.

She slipped out of the jeans, one long, lovely leg at a time. Golden realized that he was drooling, and he wiped his mouth with the back of his hand. She was standing there in front of him as naked as the day she was born. He felt as if he were looking at the goddess of love and beauty.

"Come on," she said.

"What?"

She took his hands and pulled him to his feet. Then she reached to unfasten his jeans. He shoved them down, and she dropped to her knees to finish getting them off of him. He stood there in nothing but the bottom half of a pair of long johns. Julie grabbed them by the waist and jerked them swiftly to his ankles. Golden felt his face flush as his virgin tool popped up in front of Julie's face, but he did manage to get his feet out of the long johns. Julie tossed them aside. She looked up.

She put her hands on his knees, and slowly she slid them up his thighs. He felt his tool throbbing, and then Julie put one hand under the heavy balls and with the other, she grasped the rod and squeezed it. Golden was suddenly afraid that his knees would buckle. Julie kissed the head of his prick. She took it into her mouth. Then she let it slip back out, and she stood up. Reaching for the covers on the bed, she pulled them down.

"Come on," she said. "Let's get in."

She crawled in, and while she was doing that, Golden had the most magnificent view of her ample ass that could be imagined. Reaching the other side of the bed, she rolled over on her back.

"Come on," she said.

Golden crawled in after her on his knees, his tool leading the way. He felt as if he were going to battle, and that was his main weapon. He moved over close to her, and she pulled him until he was on top of her and between her legs. He leaned forward to kiss her. He put his weight on one elbow in order to free his other hand to fondle her lovely tits. While he was thus engaged, Julie reached down to grip his rod again. It bucked in her hand. She pulled on it, and Golden let her take it where she would. Soon he felt another thrill, greater than all the others, as she guided the head of his cock into her wet slit and rubbed it up and down.

Then suddenly, she put it in just the right place and thrust her hips upward. He felt his cock slide deep into her warm, wet hole, and before he realized what he was doing, he had thrust it all the way in. He lay down on her heavily.

"Oh, Julie," he said. "That's the most wonderful thing in the whole wide world."

"Oh, yes," she said. "Yes. It is."

Slowly, savoring every minute detail, Golden withdrew until the head of his cock was on the verge of slipping free. Then he shoved it forward again, slowly and deeply. All the while, his lips pressed against hers, their tongues dueled, and with one hand he continued kneading her soft, precious tits. Julie's hands were both on his back, and she dug at his flesh with her nails. He was lucky, indeed, that she was a working woman and did not cultivate long nails. If she had, his back would have been scratched bloody.

All of a sudden, Golden was consumed with a powerful urge, and his next thrust was fast and hard, almost savage. He began pounding into her, harder and faster with each stroke, their bodies slapping together rhythmically. His breathing was heavy. With each thrust, she cried out softly.

"Uh, uh, uh, uh."

Finally, he stopped and lay heavily on her again. He was not yet spent. He was trying to catch his breath and ready himself for another round of hard thrusting. He was in the very middle of the experience of his life, and he was not thinking of anything or anyone but Julie and her wonderful body.

"Sammy?" she said.

"Hmm?"

"Let me get on top?"

"Sure," he said. "If that's what you want."

Slowly, he withdrew himself, and he rolled over onto his back. Julie got up on her knees and swung one leg over him, like she was mounting a horse. She took hold of his cock and once again, guided its path. When she had it placed just right, she lowered herself until she had taken its entire length up into her shaft. Savoring the feel, she wriggled her ass, sitting there on top of him.

"Ah," Golden moaned.

Then Julie thrust her hips forward, sliding on his hips and thighs. Forward and back, forward and back, she rode him, moving a little faster with each thrust. Soon she was riding him like a bronc. Sweat ran down her face and body onto his, already wet with its own sweat. Suddenly, with almost no warning, Golden felt the surge coming from deep inside his swollen balls.

"Oh," he said. "Oh, Julie. I'm gonna—"

With sudden and overwhelming release and relief, he felt the first spurt fire upward into her already squishy passageway, and then almost immediately the next and the next. At last, the salvo had ended. He lay there, spent and exhausted.

"Oh," he said. "Oh, I feel whipped."

"That sounds bad," she said.

"Well, it ain't. It's good. It's the best thing in the whole world. I never woulda thought I'd feel so good and so whipped at one and the same time. How do you feel?"

She smiled as she lay forward to press her breasts again on his chest.

"I feel wonderful," she said.

She pressed her lips against his for a lingering kiss. At last she rolled over, and they lay side by side.

"I love you, Julie," he said.

"And I love you, Sammy. Sammy?"

"Yes?"

"If we made a baby tonight, it'll be a strong boy, made from strong love."

"A baby?" he said.

"Well, that's how it's done," she said.

"I know, but—"

"What's the matter? Don't you want babies?"

"Course I do. With you. But we ain't got married yet. We can't be having no babies till we get married. You know what people would call them."

"I don't care what anyone says."

"Well, I do. I won't have no one talking bad about you or about our babies neither. You think we coulda really—"

"Maybe," she said. "Maybe not. You can't tell right away, but it could happen."

"Oh, golly, Julie. I got to find a way to get us to that preacher. Or else get him out here. We got to get married up. Right away. Tomorrow."

"Sammy," she said. "Relax."

"I can't relax now," he said. "Not after what you just told me. I got to think."

* * *

Slocum had not lied to old man Bradley. As late as it was, he was not sleepy. Bradley had finally turned in, but Slocum poured himself another drink and went out on the porch. He sat down there and lit a cigar, and that was the way Sam Golden found him.

"Slocum," Golden said. "I'm glad you're up."

"What's wrong, Sammy?"

"Oh, nothing, really," Golden said. "I just kinda wanted to talk to you."

He sat in the chair next to Slocum.

"Well?" Slocum said.

"What?" asked Golden, almost jumping at the sound of Slocum's voice.

"You said you wanted to talk," said Slocum. "What about?"

"Oh, that. Well, you know, me and Julie is planning on getting hitched."

"I think everyone in the valley knows that by now," said Slocum.

"Well, we don't wanta wait. We want to get it done up right away."

"This mess with Smoot ought to be settled real soon now," Slocum said. "Then—"

"I can't wait for that, Slocum. I need to get us to that preacher tomorrow. Or get him out here. I got to get it done now."

Slocum looked at Golden.

"Are you that horny, boy?" he asked.

"It ain't that," Golden said. "Slocum, this real embarrassing to talk about, and I ain't never gonna say nothing about it to no one else but only you."

"Well?"

Golden leaned toward Slocum and spoke in a low whisper.

"We already done it. Tonight."

"There's nothing wrong with that. I hope you both had a good time."

"We did, but that ain't the problem. The problem is what if—well, what if we made a baby?"

18

The next morning after breakfast, Slocum awaited a chance to speak with Julie in private. He asked her where he could find a preacher. She gave him the name of Reverend Josiah Blum and directions to Blum's house in Harleyville.

"What are you going to do?" she asked.

"I thought you'd know," he said. "Sammy told me that you all want to get hitched just as soon as possible. He said you don't want to wait till this mess is over with. I don't think it's safe for you to go to town, so I figured I'd go in there after the preacher and bring him out here. Is that all right?"

"Oh, yes," she said. "That would be wonderful. Thank you so much. But—will it be safe for you to go to town?"

"Safe as anything else I do," he said.

On his way to the corral to saddle his horse, Slocum thought about what he had said to Julie. It might not be safe. There was no telling what those Smoot men might be up to. They could be watching the road just as the ranchers were doing, and if they were to spot Slocum riding alone, they just might take a shot or two at him from ambush. What he was planning was damn foolish, and he knew it, but for some stupid reason, he felt like he had to help out the young lovers.

He rode slow and easy as he passed by the Smoot headquarters there at Golden's ranch. His eyes shifted from one side of the road to the other. He was alert to any movement, any noise. He felt strongly that he was being watched, but he saw no one. He heard nothing suspicious. No shots were fired. He made it beyond the danger spots and rode on into town.

He found the Blum residence with no trouble, and the preacher himself answered the knock on the door.

"Yes?"

"Preacher," said Slocum, "there's a young couple out at the Ringy Dingy Ranch that are really craving your services. Could you ride out there with me?"

"Well, why didn't they come in here to see me?"

"The situation with Smoot and his men is kind of tense right now," Slocum said. "It just didn't seem like a good idea. You see, the young man is one of the ranch owners."

"I see. May I ask who is the young woman?"

"Julie Bradley. Old man Bradley's daughter."

"Oh. Well, yes, of course I'll ride out there with you. Just give me a few minutes to get my things together."

Out at Smoot's headquarters, a man came bursting into the ranch house. Surprised, the nervous Smoot jumped to his feet.

"What is it?" he demanded.

"I just seen a ranny come out of Bradley's place and head towards town," the man said.

"Who was it?" Smoot asked.

"I don't know him," the man said. He shrugged. "A cowhand-looking feller."

Tarance stood up from his chair and walked over to stand close beside his boss. He was glad that Graves was out of the room. Even so, he spoke low.

"Boss," he said, "if the man went into town, he'll be coming back. We had really ought to pick them bastards off one at a time any chance we get."

"Take care of it," Smoot said.

Tarance left the room and went for a horse. Taking a Winchester rifle with him, as well as his six-gun, he rode to the front gate and on out into the road. Then he turned toward the Ringy Dingy. About half way there, he moved into the brush on the far side of the road. Taking his horse well back, he walked to the road and found himself a likely hiding place, one where he could stay well hidden, be reasonably comfortable, and be able to get off a good shot at someone riding down the road. He settled in to wait.

He was glad that he had been able to make this move without the interference of that damned Graves. He was tired of the way Graves had taken over. He had gotten this order directly from Smoot, and that was the way he liked it. He wished that Smoot had never hired Graves on in the first place. What's more, he was pretty sure that Smoot felt the same way, but now the damn Gravedigger was here, and there didn't seem to be much anyone could do about it. Nothing much but maybe a shot in the back like Smoot had already suggested. Tarance wondered if he would have the guts to try it.

Slocum did not think that even the Smoot men would shoot the preacher, but he knew they would take a shot at him if they got a chance. Back in the danger zone on the way to the Ringy Dingy, he was again alert, wary. They made it through though with no problems, and so he relaxed a bit. He and the preacher did not have much to talk about, so most of the ride was accomplished in silence. They had gotten about halfway from the Smoot hangout to the Ringy Dingy.

From his hiding place beside the road, Tarance spotted the two riders. The first one he recognized was the preacher, and that took him by surprise. Then he recognized Slocum. He started to raise his rifle, and then he remembered Graves's order to leave Slocum to him. Tarance had a moment of indecision bordering almost on panic. Here was his opportunity to kill Slocum, and he had personal reasons for wanting to do so. But if he should kill Slocum, he would have to answer to the Gravedigger. He waited until it was almost too late before he made his decision. The two riders were almost past him. He would have to step out into the road to make a back shot. In a split-second decision, he did just that, but in the process of crashing through the brush, he made enough noise to alert Slocum to the danger.

As Tarance steadied himself and raised the rifle to his shoulder, Slocum turned in his saddle, saw Tarance, and jerked out his Colt. His quick shot knocked the hat off Tarance's head, and Tarance jerked the trigger of his Winchester sending a wild shot into the air. He yelped and jumped, then turned and ran back into the brush, tearing his way through thick bramble, tripping and falling. He expected pursuit, and he scrambled desperately to his feet. He could feel the brush scratching and tearing at him as he ran, but he did not slow down.

Out in the road, Slocum entertained the idea of chasing Tarance, but only for an instant. It was more important to get the preacher safely onto the Ringy Dingy. The preacher wore an astonished and frightened look on his face.

"Merciful heavens," he said, "was that—"

"One of Smoot's men," said Slocum. "Don't worry. He wasn't after you. It was me he wanted."

"He tried to shoot you in the back," said Blum.

"He sure enough did, preacher."

"I commend you on your restraint. Most men would have killed him in your place. You simply frightened him away."

"It was a bad shot, preacher. Too quick. If I'd had another second or two, I'd have killed him all right, and glad of it."

The preacher cleared his throat, as the two rode on toward the main gate of the Ringy Dingy.

The wedding was well attended, since most of the Bradleys' neighbors were gathered up there already. It did not take long, and even though everything was hastily set up, Julie managed to have a nice ceremony and a good meal for all immediately following Reverend Blum stayed to eat and visit. He was actually fearful of the return trip to town. At last he could put it off no longer.

"Well, my friends," he announced, "I hate to leave such good company, but I'm afraid that I must be on my way home. I want to arrive before darkness sets in."

"I'll ride back in with you, preacher," Slocum said.

Blum wasn't at all sure that he wanted Slocum's company. On the one hand, he was afraid to make the trip alone. On the other hand, Slocum had said that the preacher was safe, so the chances were that if Blum went alone, there would be no shooting. But he couldn't be sure. Dave Bradley stood up and went for his hat.

"I'll go along," he said. He looked at Slocum. "All right?"

"Sure," Slocum said, glad for the company. There could be more shooting, and the return trip would be at least partially after sundown. In a few minutes, the three riders were on the way. It was a slow and tedious ride back to town, neither Slocum nor Bradley having much to say with the preacher in their company. They tensed up a bit passing the Smoot headquarters, but they got the preacher back home with no further incidents. They thanked him kindly for his services, and he hurried into the security of his own little house.

"How about a drink before we head back?" Dave said.

"Why not?" said Slocum. They rode to the saloon and left their horses at the hitch rail. Inside, they bellied up to the bar and ordered a whiskey each. They looked the room over carefully and saw no Smoot men there. The outlaws, like the ranchers, seemed to be staying together for safety reasons. When they finished their drinks, they each ordered a second.

"Hell," Dave said, "we can't make it back before dark nohow."

"You're right," said Slocum.

"Slocum?"

"Yeah?"

"I'm getting sick of this waiting around. What do you say to the idea of just getting all the men together and riding in to get those Smoot bastards? Get it over with and done."

"It has its appeal," Slocum said, "but it has some drawbacks too."

"Like what?"

"We'd lose some men," Slocum said, "and Sam's house could get messed up pretty much in a big fight like that."

"Hell, we'd all help him get it fixed back up."

"Who would fix up the ones that got killed?"

"Aw, hell, Slocum. I'm just tired of waiting around, that's all."

"So is everyone else," Slocum said. "I expect the Smoot bunch feels the same way, but the law is coming."

"Yeah, but when?"

"Tell you what, pard. If I have me just one more whiskey, I might be in a mood to accommodate you somewhat."

"What do you mean?"

"We might just go over there in the dark and play a little mischief on that Smoot bunch."

"Hey, barkeep," Dave shouted. "Two more down here."

The bartender poured the drinks, and Dave paid for them. Then he leaned over close to Slocum and spoke low.

"What you got in mind?"

"You know, they've had someone out in the bushes beside the road watching for us to ride by. That Tarance took a shot at me while I was bringing the preacher out to your place."

"Yeah?"

"You think we could find the son of a bitch out there in the dark?"

"Slocum, I growed up right out there on the Ringy Dingy. I know the whole of Whistling Valley as good as I know my own barn. We'll find him all right, or I'll kiss your ass."

They moved slowly and carefully through the brush. Slocum spotted a dark figure just ahead. He held out a hand to stop Dave, then pointed ahead. Dave looked and nodded. Slocum made another motion. The two men moved apart and then moved forward. They came up one on each side of the Smoot watchman. Slocum slipped the Colt out of its holster and held it ready. Dave did the same. Slocum cocked his, and so did Dave. The Smoot man heard the unmistakable sound, but before he could make a move, Slocum said, "Drop the rifle and raise your hands." The man did so. "Get his six-gun, Dave."

Dave moved forward and took the revolver out of the man's holster.

"We gonna kill him?" Dave asked.

"I don't know," Slocum said. "I hate to waste a bullet."

"I got a knife," said Dave. "I'll cut his fucking throat from ear to ear."

"That's awful messy."

"Well, we could hang him."

"That's better," Slocum said. "Let's do that."

"Wait a minute," the Smoot man said. "Don't do that. Don't hang me."

"Shut up," said Slocum. "Your bunch has been shooting at my back from ambush."

"I never."

"You're part of them," Slocum said. "Where's your horse?"

"He's right over there."

"Dave."

"I'll fetch it," said Dave.

Dave moved off to bring the horse, and Slocum said to the man, "Get your clothes off."

"What?"

"You heard me. Get them off."

When Dave returned with the horse, the man was stark naked. Slocum made him mount the horse, and then he tied the man's hands to the saddle horn. With their prisoner secure, Slocum went back for his Appaloosa and Dave's horse. He mounted his own and led Dave's back to where Dave and the trembling prisoner waited. Then they led the naked horseman to the main gate of Golden's ranch, the ranch where Smoot and his gang were ensconced.

Slocum took his rope and fashioned a hangman's knot. He tossed the knot up over the sign that was overhead and across the gateway. Then he tied the other end of the rope to the fence. Dave took the noose and slipped it over the naked man's head.

"No. No!" the man screamed.

"Shut up," Slocum said, "or I'll slap your horse on his ass. You hear me?"

"Don't slap him," the man said. "I'll shut up."

"I got a few questions," said Slocum. "You give me the right answers, and we won't slap that horse. All right?"

"Yeah. I'll tell you anything."

"Are there anymore like you out here along the road?"

"No, sir. I was the only one. Smoot just puts out one each night."

"How many gun hands has Smoot got left?"

"I ain't for sure. Maybe a half a dozen. But one of them's that there Gravedigger, and he's a mean one."

"Does Smoot know the law's coming? A whole posse? How the hell does he think he's going to get away with all this?"

"Well, he just thinks he can get all the deeds before the law gets here," the man said. "Then he'll tell the law that all the killing was Bradley's doing."

"Does he think he can get away with that?" said Dave.

"He says if he's got the deeds then he's got the power, and the law will be on his side."

"You got a relief man coming?" Slocum asked.

"Not till morning."

"Well, Dave," said Slocum, "I'm craving me another glass of whiskey. Let's ride on out of here."

"You gonna let me down?" the Smoot man said.

"We're gonna do you a big favor," Dave said. "We ain't gonna slap your horse."

"If you're lucky," said Slocum, "he won't decide to walk out from under you before your relief man shows up."

"But—but my hands is tied to the saddle."

"Hey, that's right," Dave said. "If the horse walks away, he won't walk out from under this ole boy. He can't. What'll happen?"

"I guess when that rope stretches tight, it'll just pull his head off," Slocum said.

"Oh, hell," said Dave. "That's sickening. Let's go. I don't want to see that."

"All right," said Slocum. "Let's go."

They turned and rode toward the Ringy Dingy, the naked man in the saddle screaming at them for mercy. He finally stopped when he knew they were gone. He sat there in the saddle helpless. He was naked, a noose was around his neck, and his hands were tied to the saddle horn. He tried to think of a way out of his dilemma, but he could think of nothing save waiting for his relief and hoping that horse stood still all that time. He couldn't stop thinking about what Slocum had said. If the horse should move forward, it would pull him with it by his hands, but then the noose would tighten around his neck. He would be pulled forward by his hands and backward by his neck. Shit, he thought, the son of a bitch was right. His head would be pulled clean off. He talked to his horse trying to keep it calm and steady.

He had no idea how long he had been sitting there when the horse did start to walk slowly forward.

"Ho. Wait. Steady there, old boy."

The horse kept walking.

"Stop. Stop, God damn it. Whoa."

It kept walking. Damn, there was a lot of slack in that rope. With every slow step of the horse, the man expected to feel the noose tightening around his neck, but it did not. At last the horse stopped at the edge of the lane. He had found some grass to nibble on. The man breathed a sigh of relief. But he was not yet out of danger. He knew that. The damned horse could take it in his mind to move again at any time.

At last his relief came riding up, and his neck had not yet been stretched. He was mightily relieved, but then he realized his total predicament. The relief man would see him in his terribly embarrassing situation. He flushed over his entire body.

"Haw," the new man shouted as he rode up. "Gawdamn, dumb butt, what happened to you?"

"Don't ask no stupid questions," the naked man said. "Just get me a-loose from here."

19

Sam Golden came out of Julie's bedroom just before breakfast for the second time, but this time he did not have to go out through the back window. Julie had already gone to the kitchen. When Golden made his first appearance of the day, Dave Bradley, old man Bradley and Slocum were already seated at the table, drinking coffee. As soon as Golden stepped out of the bedroom, feeling that all eyes were on him, Dave called out in a loud voice, "Look at the shit-eating grin on that boy's face. I reckon we all know what he's been up to."

Golden felt himself blush from the top of his head clear down to his toes. He was glad that all anyone could see of him was his red face. He thought for an instant about turning around and going right back into the bedroom and shutting the door and staying there until the rest had all eaten and gone their ways, but he knew that wouldn't do. He would just have to tough it out. Looking down at the floor, he walked over to the table and took his seat.

"Good morning," he muttered.

"Good morning, Sammy," Slocum said. He had some other things in mind to say, but he decided that he would not join Dave in his youthful teasing.

Just then Julie came out of the kitchen bringing coffee to Golden.

"Good morning, Mrs. Golden," Slocum said.

Julie smiled as she put the coffee in front of her new husband.

"Thank you," Golden said.

"I'm surprised as hell that either one of you two was able to get outa bed this morning," Dave said. "I bet neither one of you got a wink a sleep last night. Hell, I bet you was—"

"That's enough, Dave," old Bradley said.

"Breakfast will be out in just a few minutes," Julie said, ignoring her brother. She turned and hurried back into the kitchen.

"Aw, I'm just funning with them," Dave said with a pout. "Hell, ain't no harm in it is there?"

"Well, you done it, and it was enough," the old man said. "The funning's over with and done."

"Well, then, speaking a fun," Dave said, "let me tell you what me and ole Slocum here done last night while the rest of you was all at home and in bed." He looked at his father. "It's a whole different matter, and it ain't got nothing to do with wedding nights."

He then proceeded to tell the entire tale of the naked near-hanging. Everyone around the table got a big laugh. Even Golden was not so embarrassed that he couldn't enjoy the story. When they at last stopped laughing, old Bradley was wiping tears from his eyes with his napkin. He caught his breath finally enough to speak.

"So," he said, "do you reckon the son of a bitch got his head popped off?"

"We got no idea," Dave said. "We just rode off and left him like that."

The table roared with laughter again, and Julie came out of the kitchen.

"What am I missing?" she asked.

Dave told the whole tale again, and everyone, including Julie, roared again with laughter. Julie went back to the kitchen just as the front door opened and Sally came into the house. She took off her hat and hung it on the tree beside the door. Then she moved over to the table and took a seat. She sat down heavily and with a deep sigh.

"Long night?" Slocum asked her, knowing that she had

taken a turn at night-riding the herd the night before. He had offered to do it for her, but she had insisted that she could do her part as well as any of the men. Some of the cattle, after all, were hers. He did not argue with her further.

"Not bad," she said. "Everything was quiet out there."

"Not where we were," Dave said, and there was another round of laughter. Sally gave him an inquisitive look, and Julie came out of the kitchen with a platter. Sally stood up.

"Let me help you bring that stuff out," she said.

"No, sir," said Dave, "things wasn't quiet where we was at, was they, Slocum?"

Slocum smiled and shook his head. "No, they weren't," he said.

When the breakfast platters were all laid out and the coffee cups all refilled, Julie and Sally took their seats at the table.

"Now," Sally said, "tell me what you're talking about last night."

Dave told the tale for the third time, and if anything, the roar of the small crowd was greater than it had been for the first two tellings. Of course, the tale was embellished some with each new telling. Their hapless victim's whimperings and pleadings, his shiverings, and his ludicrous naked appearance were given new and more detailed description. Finally, fearful of letting their breakfasts cool, everyone decided to get serious and get busy eating. It almost worked, but now and then someone at the table would recall the tale and break into renewed raucous laughter, which the others then, of course, could not resist joining.

Tarance brought Bart into the big ranch house to see Smoot. Poor Bart was the man who had been stripped and strung up the night before. It was his second such humiliation at the hands of the ranchers, and he was wanting to quit his job and get the hell out of the valley. Tarance had told him that he had better have a talk with Smoot first.

"You just ride outa here like that without no word, there ain't no telling what that gravediggin' bastard might do," he had said.

In the ranch house, Tarance walked over to where Smoot

was sitting behind the desk. Bart dragged along behind somewhat reluctantly. He really did not want to be there. Smoot looked up at the two men and leaned back in his chair, folding his hands behind his head.

"You heard what happened to Bart last night?" Tarance asked.

He glanced over at P. T. Graves, who was sitting in a far corner of the room sipping coffee. He would much rather have caught Smoot alone but that seemed increasingly difficult to accomplish.

"I heard," Smoot said.

"It's the second time," Bart said. "The second time they done that to me. It's downright embarrassing. And this time it was even worser. For one thing, I couldn't even run and hide. And then, I coulda easy been killed. Mr. Smoot, I want to get outa here. I want to go somewhere where no one's even heard about none of this humiliating stuff."

"What kind of a chickenshit are you?" said Graves in a quiet, cold voice from his dark corner of the room.

"What?"

"You heard me. If a man had done me that way, I'd kill him. I wouldn't stop till I'd finished the job."

"Well, that's easy for you to say," Bart said. "I can't go up against a man like that. You can. You can go up against him."

"I can take him too," said Graves. "But there are other ways to get a man than facing him. If I was as helpless as you, I'd at least stick around and help out those who are going to even the score for you."

"I don't care about that," Bart said. "I just want to get as far away from that mean-minded son of a bitch as I possibly can. I don't never want nothing like that to happen to me again. And I sure don't want to get my ass killed."

"Stick around, Bart," Smoot said. "I won't put you out by yourself like that again. You'll be safe enough."

"When I kill Slocum," the Gravedigger said, "I'll even let you piss on the body."

"And if I just ride on out?"

"I'll kill you."

"Well, all right. If I don't have to go out there by myself no more."

"I guarantee it," Smoot said.

Tarance and Bart left the house, and Graves stood up slowly and deliberately and walked over to stand in front of Smoot, who was seated behind the desk.

"You know what they're up to?" he asked.

"Tarance and Bart?"

"No, the God damned ranchers."

"Oh. No. Do you?"

"They're not waiting for those lawmen to show up," the Gravedigger said. "They're moving in on us. That business last night was calculated to make us nervous. It almost lost us one man. It could still lose us men. When the others hear about it, some of them might run out on us. Bart still might run out. Slip away in the night. We got to make some kind of move. Right now. We got to be in clear control of the valley before the deputy marshals get here."

"Well, how do we do that?" Smoot asked. "We can't just attack the Ringy Dingy. All the ranchers are gathered up there, and they outnumber us."

"We have to get rid of Slocum," said Graves. "Without him, they're nothing. We could take them in spite of their numbers. And if he's out of the way, their numbers would be smaller,'cause some of them would break and run."

"What do you propose?"

"Give me a paper and pen."

Graves pulled up a chair to the desk, and when Smoot handed him paper, pen and inkwell, he dipped the pen in the ink and started to write.

"Old friend Slocum," he wrote, "we find ourselves on opposite sides this time. It seems to me that you are the one holding the ranchers together over there, and I, of course, am the strength of this camp. I propose that you and I meet face to face in Harleyville this evening at six o'clock. I will be there waiting for you. I promise you that I will have no one backing my play. It will be just you and me. If you do not show up, I will spread the word all over the west that you are a great chickenshit. I look forward to our meeting. Your old pard, P. T. Graves."

When he had finished his note, he shoved it across the desk. Smoot picked it up and read it. He looked at Graves with amazement.

"You mean to do this?" he asked.

"I do."

"Just like you said here? Alone?"

"Alone," said Graves. "I don't need help. There's not a man alive I can't outshoot. And Slocum is an honorable man. If he shows, he'll show alone. I'll kill him. As soon as that's done, we can move against the ranchers."

"Yeah," said Smoot. "You're right. We can run them all out. All except old Bradley. We'll have to kill him. But with no witnesses, the law will have to listen to our version of what happened here. Yeah. But how are you going to get this here note to Slocum?"

"We'll send Tarance over there under a flag of truce."

Tarance rode onto the Ringy Dingy with a great deal of trepidation. He was carrying a white flag on the end of a stick, but he wasn't at all sure it would be honored. His eyes darted nervously from here to there as he rode the long path from the main gate to the ranch house. Dave Bradley, already mounted, saw him, pulled out his Winchester and rode toward him fast. Tarance stopped and held both his hands high.

"Don't shoot," he called out. "See this here flag?"

"What are you up to?" Dave asked.

"I ain't here to start no trouble," Tarance said. "Not by myself I sure ain't. I been sent to deliver a message."

"All right. What is it?"

"It's in my pocket. It's wrote down and sealed, and I'm supposed to hand it direct to Slocum."

"Let me have it," said Dave. "I'll take it to him."

"I was give real strong orders that I got to hand it direct to Slocum."

Dave thought a moment. He did not like the idea of escorting Tarance to the ranch house, but then, what harm could the man do? He was alone, like he said. He'd be a fool to start anything.

"All right," he said. "Come on."

As Tarance rode on toward the ranch house, Dave fell in behind him, still holding his rifle ready. Slocum spotted them coming and waited on the porch. Close to the porch, Tarance did not get out of the saddle. He pulled the paper out of his pocket and held it out toward Slocum.

"I was told to bring you this," he said.

Slocum stepped down off the porch and walked out to Tarance. He took the letter, broke the seal and read it.

"Can I go now?" said Tarance.

"I should blast you outa your saddle," said Dave.

"Let him go," Slocum said.

"All right," said Dave. "Get going and feel damn lucky."

He watched to make sure that Tarance did indeed ride through the gate and turn back toward Smoot's hangout. Then he put his rifle away and climbed down out of the saddle. He stepped over to Slocum.

"What the hell is it?" he asked.

"It's a personal challenge from the Gravedigger," Slocum said. "He wants to meet me in Harleyville this evening for a showdown."

"You going?"

"Yeah. It's a chance to knock out our biggest problem."

"I'll go with you."

"No," Slocum said. "He says he's going to be alone. He wants me to ride in the same way."

"You trust that snake?"

"I know him," Slocum said. "There's some ways I wouldn't trust him. But when he says he'll face a man alone for a gunfight, he means it. He's got too much pride to do it any other way."

"Well, I don't like it," Dave said. "Hell, Slocum, can you take him?"

Slocum thought for a moment. "I don't know," he said. "I reckon we'll find out though."

*   *   *

Slocum saddled his Appaloosa, mounted up and headed for town. He had not told anyone where he was going or what he was planning to do. And he had told Dave to keep his mouth shut about it as well. He meant to accept the Gravedigger's challenge on the Gravedigger's terms. It was a long and lonely ride for Slocum, for he was thinking all the way in that it could very well be his last. He had seen the Gravedigger in action. The man was fast, fast as lightning or a snake's strike. And he was accurate. In short, he was a deadly son of a bitch. Perhaps the worst Slocum had ever seen.

"What the hell is he up to?" old Bradley asked Dave.

"I ain't supposed to tell," Dave said.

"What the hell do you mean by that? Is he running out on us?"

"He wouldn't do that," Golden said. "He wouldn't run on us."

"Well, what's the damn big secret then?"

"Oh, all right," said Dave. "I'll tell you, but he told me to stay here and not to let on what was going on. So when I tell you, you all got to stay right here and wait for him to get back. That's all."

"So tell," snapped old Bradley.

"Slocum got this here challenge from Graves," Dave said.

"What kind of a challenge?" asked Sally.

"To meet him in town at six, face to face, each man alone."

"A gunfight?" Sally said.

"That's right."

"God damn," old Bradley said. "Can he take that Gravedigger?"

"Slocum's damn good," Golden said, "but even he says that Graves is one of the best he ever saw."

"Can he take him?"

"I don't know."

"We shouldn't let him face that killer alone," old Bradley said.

"We got no choice," said Dave. "He made me promise."

Sally thought to herself, it's a matter of man's honor. Slocum would feel like his honor had been smirched if any of these men went in to help him out. And the man who did it would be ashamed that he had ruined a friendship. Hell, they'd let him get himself killed over that foolish notion. Not only that, but with Slocum killed, the ranchers would never stand up to the Smoot bunch. They would throw away everything for that honor.

Well, she wouldn't. It was nothing to her. Slocum was going to ride away from her one of these days anyhow. What difference if he rode away hating her, but alive? She said nothing, but she went into the house and into her room. She found her Winchester and checked it. Then she walked through the house and out the back door. The others were all gathered out on the porch. She made her way to the corral and caught up and saddled her favorite horse. With the Winchester in a saddle scabbard, she headed for the main gate, but she did not ride directly down the lane. She rode around. If anyone back at the ranch house were to see her, she would have a good start on them.

20

At the Ringy Dingy ranch house, Dave Bradley paced the length of the big front porch. Slocum had gone to town for a showdown with the Gravedigger. Dave couldn't help thinking that it was showdown time all the way around. No matter what happened in town, he thought, the Smoot crowd would think it was time to make their big move. If Slocum should kill Graves, they would be desperate and panic. If it happened the other way around, they would think that with Slocum out of the way, the ranchers would be easy pickings. They would make their move. To Dave's way of thinking, the ranchers needed to make that move first. Old man Bradley stepped out onto the porch.

"What's wrong with you, Dave?" he asked. "Pull up a chair and settle down."

As the old man took a seat, Dave pulled a chair over close to him and sat. He leaned forward intently.

"Listen," he said. "That gunfight that Slocum has rode into town to do. It's gonna set the whole thing off. Slocum and Graves has lit the fuse. Do you understand what I'm saying?"

Old Bradley rubbed his chin and rocked his chair back on its hind legs.

"Yeah," he said. "I think I do, boy. You got ideas?"

"I say let's get all the fighting men together and ride over to Sammy's place and take it. I say let's do it now before that Smoot bunch takes it in mind to do the same thing to us. It's gonna happen one way or the other, and it's gonna happen today. Let's let it be us that makes that first move."

Old Bradley slapped his leg and stood up. "Let's do it," he said. "We can't let Slocum do all our fighting for us. Gather up the men."

P. T. Graves sat alone at a window beside a table in a cafe in Harleyville sipping coffee and watching the traffic out on the street. He felt certain that Slocum would ride in and that he would be alone. He felt as certain that he would kill Slocum, but Slocum was better than most he had done away with. He was looking forward to the contest. He was early. He had planned it that way. He wanted time to relax. He wanted to be there waiting calmly when Slocum rode in. What would come next was in the back of his mind: the taking over of the whole valley, and then his own taking over of the entire Smoot operation. It would be all right to be king of the valley, he thought, but it was best to keep his mind on the business at hand. With Slocum buried, there would be plenty of time to think about the other stuff.

Slocum was worried. He admitted as much to himself. He knew there was a good chance that this was his last day on earth. He meant to stand face to face with Graves. It was the only way he knew how to fight. It would have made sense to have brought along some backup. Dave had volunteered. It would make sense to slip up behind Graves. But Slocum did not fight that way. Riding into Harleyville, he tried to think of ways to give himself some kind of edge, get the sun in Graves's face, say something to rattle Graves just before the draw, fling himself to the ground to one side at the last instant. Graves knew all those tricks.

He stopped the big Appaloosa just across the street from the cafe in which Graves was sitting, and he could see the black-suited gunslinger through the front window. He saw the man sitting there calmly sipping coffee. Dismounting, he lapped the reins of his horse around the hitch rail. He turned to watch Graves and to wait. He knew that Graves would let him wait for at least a few minutes. It was all a part of the game, calculated to make Slocum nervous. Well, it wasn't needed. He was already about as nervous as he could get. He wished the son of a bitch would get up and come on out in the street to get it over with one way or the other. He wouldn't let it get to him though. He could stand there and wait as long as Graves took to make his decision.

Tarance burst through the front door of the ranch house, startling Smoot. "The ranchers is coming!" he shouted. "Our watchman just come riding up here to tell me."

"Get all the men in here," Smoot said. He rushed to his gun cabinet and took out a Henry rifle. Checking its load, he hurried over to the front door and stepped out onto the porch, squinting his eyes toward the gate. He saw no one. Tarance came running back, followed by the rest of the gang. They gathered up on the porch behind Smoot.

"Where are they?" Smoot asked.

"They'll show up any minute now," the man who had been on lookout said.

"How do you know they're coming here?" asked Smoot. "Maybe they're headed for town to help Slocum."

"I don't think so," Tarance said. "Slocum wouldn't allow it. He's like Graves that way."

"They looked to me like they was headed to war," the other man said.

"Hey," said Tarance. "Here they come."

"I can see," Smoot said. "Get in the house. All of you. Get ready for anything."

Once the others had all gone in, Smoot backed himself up to the door to wait. He did not think they would gun him down without some preliminary talk. The riders came close, and Smoot recognized old man Bradley riding alongside his son at the head of the group. He made a quick count and estimated that a dozen men or so made up this band. He was a bit relieved at that. He had been afraid there would be twenty or more, but then, some of the ranchers were old farts, and even of those who could and would mount up and fight, the Bradleys likely couldn't get them all together at once. They stopped, and old Bradley rode forward a few feet.

"Smoot," Bradley called out. "Get all your men out here and throw down all your guns."

"You must be crazy," Smoot said. "Why the hell would I do something that foolish?"

"If you don't," Bradley said, "we'll blast you out of there."

"You can try," Smoot said, and he quickly ducked into the house. "Start shooting, men," he yelled, and he himself ran across the room and got behind the big desk. The men at the front windows cut loose, almost immediately filling the air in the room with smoke and the smell of gunpowder. The noise made Smoot cringe. But shots were returned. Bullets crashed through windows and shattered various objects in the room. Smoot got down on his knees behind the desk.

Back in Harleyville, Slocum watched as Graves stood up, took some coins out of his pocket and tossed them on the table. Then he turned and walked, disappearing from Slocum's view. Slocum waited for the Gravedigger to come out the front door, but he did not immediately appear. Another ploy. Another trick to work on Slocum's nerves. Let him think you're coming, then pause a while. All right, Slocum thought. Two can play that game. He walked down the street to the general store and stepped inside.

"Can I help you?" the man said.

"You got any good cigars?"

"Right over here."

Slocum stepped to the counter to examine the wares. He made a careful selection, paid for it, then took out a match and struck it. He held the flame to the tip of the cigar and puffed. When he had it going good, he shook the match to put it out. The man behind the counter shoved an ash tray toward him, and he dropped the match stick into the tray.

"Thanks," he said.

"You come back now," the man said.

"I hope so," said Slocum, and he walked to the door and stepped back out onto the street. Graves was standing in front of the cafe. The Gravedigger turned his head toward Slocum.

"There you are," he said. He sounded calm enough. "I was afraid you'd changed your mind and run off."

"Not a chance," said Slocum. There was too much distance between them for a fight with revolvers. Slocum stood still and puffed his cigar.

"There was a time we fought side by side. Remember?"

"I remember," said Slocum. "You were fighting on the right side that time."

"The money was right. What's in this fight for you anyway?"

"Nothing," Slocum said. "Not a damn thing."

"I didn't think you that big a fool."

"Yeah? Well, nothing about you surprises me. You're right where I'd expect you to be—mixed in with a bunch of cowards, land thieves and frauds. Scaring women, children and old men. Dry-gulching innocent folks. No surprise there."

"I'm going to kill you, Slocum."

"You can try. It's your move."

"You know I can beat you," Graves said. "I'll give you the first move."

He stepped slowly down into the street and started walking toward Slocum. Slocum walked to the middle of the street and turned to face Graves. He stood still.

As soon as the first shots came at them from the ranch house, the Bradleys, Golden and the other ranchers reacted quickly, some of them firing back at the house from horseback, others dismounting and running for cover. One man fell from his horse hit badly. A slug tore through the flesh of old Bradley's left arm. He cursed, fired a shot at the house and got down off his horse, running toward an old barrel. Dave Bradley stood up behind a wagon in the yard and fired a shot at one of the windows. The outlaw behind it howled and dropped. Suddenly the shooting stopped almost as suddenly as it had started.

"We got us a standoff here," Bradley said to Dave.

"We got to find a way to get them out of there," Dave said. "I'll try to reason with them."

"Don't show yourself."

"Hey, Smoot," Bradley called out. "Smoot. You hear me?"

"I hear you. What do you want?"

"I want to give you one more chance. Throw out your guns and come out with your hands up. No one else will get hurt. I promise you."

"I'll make you an offer," Smoot called out. "You men get on your horses and ride out of here, and no one will shoot. We'll let you ride offa my place here without getting killed. What do you say?"

"We ain't leaving till you're out of there or dead."

"Then quit talking and get to shooting," Smoot yelled.

Immediately shots came from the house. The ranchers out in the yard all ducked behind what cover they had. A few returned fire.

"I wish those damn lawmen would show up," Bradley said.

"Hell," said Dave, "they wouldn't make that much difference."

"I'm afraid they can hold out in there longer than we can out here. Likely they got plenty of ammunition in there. They got food and water too."

"And bandages and stuff," Dave said, glancing at his father's bloody arm. "We could send a man back for supplies and reinforcements."

Not far away, Sam Golden listened to the conversation of the Bradleys. He looked around himself, found a broken handle on the ground, scrambled over to it, grabbed it up and scurried back to his hiding place. Not far off was a pile of straw. Golden ran over there and ducked behind it, just dodging a couple of bullets that were sent after him from the house. Behind the straw, he pulled off his shirt. Stuffing the shirt with straw, he wrapped the bundle tightly around the handle and tied it tight. Dave Bradley noticed his antics.

"What are you up to, Sam?" Dave called out.

"A faster way to get those bastards outa there," Golden said. "Who's got a match?"

"I got some," said Dave.

"Can you toss them over here?"

"I'll bring them to you."

Crouching low, Dave ran. A bullet nicked his leg, and he jumped and rolled, coming up beside Golden.

"Damn," he said.

"You all right?"

"Yeah. It ain't nothing." He dug some matches out of his pocket and handed them to Golden. "Here," he said. "Just what the hell are you up to?"

"I'm going to set fire to that house."

"Hell, Sammy, it's your house."

"I wouldn't move Julie in there after that bunch had been in it for so long," Golden said. "It ain't a fit place no more. I'll build us a new house."

"We'll all help you."

"Besides, if that's my place, I reckon I have a right to burn it down, don't I?"

"I'd say so."

Golden struck a match and held it to the bundle tied to the end of the handle. It caught.

"Now what?" Dave asked.

"I've got to run up there and toss this thing where it'll do some good."

"Hey, boys," Dave called out. "Cover Sammy."

Golden stood and ran toward the house, and all of the ranchers fired at the windows of the house, keeping the outlaws inside ducking down. At the side wall of the house, Golden found some loose and rotting boards. He held the torch to them until the flames began to lick at the wall. Then he stepped back and tossed the torch onto the roof. He thought for an instant, then ran around to the back of the house. Some of them might try to get out that way. He found a new hiding place and waited.

"You going to go for that gun, Slocum?" said Graves.

"After you. You're the one called this party."

People were gathered on both sides of the street. The only clear spots were those behind the two combatants. Kids peeked out from behind men's legs or women's skirts. Faces were pressed against all windows in town. There were even men on rooftops looking down, anxiously waiting to see the blood fly.

Graves stretched his fingers, then clenched his fists and opened them again. He's fixing to make his move, thought Slocum. This is it.

To the people watching, both hands seemed to move at once, but only one shot rang out. It was loud, like a rifle shot. Graves's six-gun was only halfway up when he stopped still. Slocum raised his the rest of the way and pointed at Graves's chest. He did not fire. Something was wrong. Graves was standing still and blood was running down his shirt from a hole in his chest. Slocum stood confused. Then Graves fell forward, his face bouncing on the hard dirt street.

Slocum looked around trying to figure out where the shot had come from. He knew that he had not fired. He could see no clue. He moved quickly to where the Gravedigger lay still, and he saw that the shot had entered Graves's back. He rolled over the body. Graves was dead.

"Damn it," he said.

A man stepped down from the sidewalk.

"What happened?" he asked.

"Someone got him in the back," Slocum said.

"Well, it don't seem to matter much. He's dead, and that won't hurt no feelings around here. Smoot's maybe."

"Yeah," Slocum said. Still, he wondered where the rifle shot had come from. He studied the angle of the shot, where it had entered the back and where it had exited the front. It must have been Dave, he thought. No one else knew of the meeting. But Dave had promised that he would not interfere. The shot had come from almost directly behind Graves, Slocum figured. But it had come from above. He stepped back and looked up toward the roof of the building there. He saw a couple of observers there.

"Hey, up there," he called.

"Yeah?"

"Anyone up there fire a shot?"

"Nope."

Slocum noticed that the building had a second floor window, and he could see that the window was open. The shot must have been fired from that window. He went inside the place, a haberdashery.

"What's upstairs?" he asked.

"Just a storeroom."

Slocum looked around and saw the stairs. He ran to the

stairs and up them. The room was empty, but on the floor by the open window, he found a spent rifle shell. A .45. Likely fired from a Winchester. He picked it up and dropped it into his pocket. On his way back down the stairs, he asked himself why it meant so much to him to find out who had killed Graves. Whoever it was had most likely saved his life. Back in the store below, he asked, "Did you see anyone go up there a while ago?"

"If anyone was up there, he sneaked by me. Wouldn'ta been a problem. I was watching you and that other one out in the street."

Slocum went to the back door and stepped out behind. There were fresh hoofprints just outside the door. The killer had ridden up there and slipped inside, then gone up the stairs and taken the position at the window. That seemed probable. But there was no telling who it might have been. He still considered Dave. On the other hand, there might be plenty of folks in town who, when they saw what was going on, might have taken the opportunity to do away with the Gravedigger. He decided that he might never know, and he had just as well go on back to the ranch.

Flames were on the left and behind Smoot and his men. The roof overhead was smoldering.

"We have to get out of here," Tarance said.

"We can't get out the back," said Smoot. "It's all aflame back there. We'll have to go out the front door blasting our way."

"We could give it up."

"You want to hang?"

One of the men said, "I'll take my chance." He tossed his weapons out one of the broken front windows and went through the front door holding his hands high, staggering and coughing. The others followed him, all except Smoot and Tarance.

"We got to do something," said Tarance.

"If we go out there shooting, we'll be cut to pieces."

"If we give up, we'll hang, and if we stay here, we'll burn to death."

"Well, I say we go out shooting," Smoot said.

"There's one other chance," said Tarance. "If we move fast enough, we might be able to get through that wall of flames behind us and get out the back door."

"You want to try it?"

"Watch me."

Tarance buried his face in his left arm and, holding a revolver in his right hand, ran toward where he thought the back door was located. He hit it hard, crashed through into the open air, saw that his shirt had caught fire, saw Sam Golden out there with a gun. He screamed and snapped off a shot at Golden. Golden fired back. Tarance twitched, lay still and burned. Golden walked around the house. No one else would get out that back way, not without burning the way Tarance had done—or worse. Just as he rounded the corner of the house and saw that the ranchers had some prisoners, Smoot ran screaming and shooting out onto the porch. Six ranchers, including both Bradleys, fired at once. Smoot staggered, twisted, and fell off the porch headlong.

Old man Bradley looked at his son.

"It's over," he said.

"What about Tarance?"

"I got him around back," said Golden. "What about Slocum?"

"And Graves," said Dave.

"All right," Bradley said. "Let's have a couple of men ride back to the ranch and let everyone there know how things came out."

"All the wounded," said Dave, "and that includes you."

"All right. The rest take these prisoners on into town and lock them up. Find out what happened with Slocum and Graves."

Dave and Golden rode at the head of the group of ranchers going into Harleyville.

"I sure do hope Slocum's all right," Golden said.

"If he ain't," said Dave, "the rest of us will take care of that Gravedigger once and for all."

"Hey, someone's coming at us."

"Slow it down, men," said Dave. "Why, that's Sally."

The riders stopped when they met Sally, and she stopped as well.

"Sally," Dave said. "Where you been?"

"I went into Harleyville."

"Slocum—"

"He's just fine," she said. "Say, don't tell him you seen me here. All right?"

"Well, all right," said Dave. "If that's how you want it. Men?"

"We won't say nothing."

"I never seen a thing."

"So where'd you get these men?" Sally asked.

"We whipped the whole Smoot crowd," said Dave. "These here all that's left alive."

"Smoot?"

"He's dead."

"Then it's really all over?"

"It's over, Sally."

"I'll be damned. I can go home and stay."

"We all can," said one of the ranchers.

"Well, right now, I think I'll go on back to your place. Maybe start packing my things."

"We got to take these prisoners in," Dave said. "Soon as we get them locked up, we'll be headed back."

"See you soon," said Sally.

Slocum felt like he ought to do something. After all, he was sort of responsible for the body in the street. There was no law in Harleyville to report anything to, and the undertaker had already brought his wagon out to load up the carcass. Slocum went to where his Appaloosa waited patiently and unloosed the reins from the rail. He was about to mount up when he saw the four riders coming into town. Something about their look made him pause. They stopped in front of the saloon, tied their horses and went inside. Slocum walked on over there.

He found the four men bellied up to the bar, wetting their whistles after their journey, and he walked over to stand beside them. It was then that he saw one of the badges. He was right.

"You the deputies from the capital?" he asked.

"That's right," said one of the four.

"My name's Slocum. I been working with the ranchers, Bradley and them."

"Glad to meet you, Slocum. We were told to get with Bradley."

"I'll take you out to him," Slocum said. "Along the way, I can fill you in one what just happened here in town."

They finished their drinks and went outside. They were about to mount up when Slocum stopped them.

"Hold on a minute," he said. "Here comes Dave Bradley and some more of the ranchers."

They met the ranchers in front of the jail. The prisoners were all locked in a cell.

"Now maybe someone can tell us what's going on," said a deputy.

"Why don't we do that over a drink?" Dave said. "There ain't no hurry now."

Back in the saloon, seated at a table with a bottle and glasses, Dave said, "You fellas got here just in time to clean up after everything. The fighting's over. Smoot's dead. All of his men that didn't get killed are locked up in the jailhouse. And, uh, say, Slocum, what about Graves?"

"Dead," said Slocum.

"Then all we have to do is write up a report and take those prisoners back to the capital with us."

"That's about it."

For moment, everyone sipped their drinks. No one talked. Then Golden spoke up, looking at Slocum with admiration.

"So you beat the Gravedigger," he said.

"No," Slocum said. "I didn't. Someone got him from behind. I don't know who it was."

Dave thought that he knew, but he kept his mouth shut. He had promised.

"So what now, Slocum?" Dave said.

"Oh, I don't know. I might—"

"Stick around for a while," said Golden. "Hell. I got to get my ranch back in shape and working, and I got to build a new house."

"Sally could use some more help too, I reckon," Dave said. "And we'll have the roundup before long. You might as well—"

"Stick around for a while," Slocum said. "I guess."

Watch for

SLOCUM'S WARPATH

276th novel in the exciting SLOCUM series
from Jove

Coming in February!